Venus and her prey

This is an engrossing novel of sexual tension and jealousy, set among the English upper classes during one perfect English summer.

Juliet—cool, lithe and modern—comes from Oxford as au pair to Gerald, Monica and their two children, in their beautiful old country home. Gerald is the local squire; devoted husband and dedicated amorist. Monica, secure of her place in his heart and home, makes it her business to know, and not mind, about his incessant affairs on the side. But when Gerald starts to fancy Juliet—beautiful, casual Juliet—forever sunbathing in the baking sunshine among the yew hedges of the formal garden—Monica's complaisance crumbles. She asks Gerald not to pursue Juliet, but Gerald cannot resist: and so for the first time in their lives, he embarks on an affair which he keeps secret from his wife.

But Monica knows. She tries to control her jealousy, but the sexual contentment radiating from the two of them is unendurable. Other elements in her torment are the children, Harriet and Martin, dimly aware of the undercurrents and both frightened and elated by them; and Gerald's domineering mother, Mrs Webster, who visits them and malevolently stirs the trouble she sees brewing.

As the tranquil life of the countryside flows on—picnics, village fêtes, church and Sunday lunch—and as the sun pours down on the cornfields and the fountain splashes on the terrace, Monica's silent rage and misery grow and fester.

In Polly Hobson's dazzling book, the tension builds as remorselessly as the dark forces of passion and hatred beneath the surface of the perfect summer days. The story is memorably vivid, and totally absorbing.

Also by Polly Hobson

Brought up in Bloomsbury (1959)
Murder won't out (1964)
Titty's dead (1968)
The three graces (1970)

For children
The mystery house (1963)

Venus and her prey

Polly Hobson

Constable London

First published in Great Britain 1975
by Constable and Company Ltd
10 Orange Street London WC2H 7EG
Copyright © 1975 by Polly Hobson

ISBN 0 09 460850 4

Set in Intertype Baskerville

Printed in Great Britain by
The Barleyman Press Ltd
Bristol

the corner of the peacock. Their stares bored into her.

"All right," she said, giving in and sitting up. "What is it?"

They were standing side by side. Harriet was dark and Martin fair but they were unmistakeably brother and sister. They had the same thin bones and fine hair, both stared with the same penetrating eyes. They were barefoot and dressed in nothing but small cotton shorts.

"You look like the picture in my Fairy Book," Harriet said. "Yellow hair and blue eyes. I coloured her in."

"I'm going to marry Juliet," Martin announced.

"You can't, you're only six."

"Yes I can."

"No you can't. Besides you're going to marry me."

"Brothers and sisters don't get married. But anyway Martin can't marry me till he's grown up and by then he probably won't want to, he'll like someone else better."

"No I shan't."

"Where's Mummy?" Harriet said, looking sideways, wanting to make absolutely sure.

"She's gone out to tea."

"*We* think it would be nice to get wet in the fountain. We're boiled."

Juliet knew nothing about children but the note in Harriet's voice gave her to beware. After only a few days the atmosphere of the place had made itself felt. The house had been in the family for generations and had imposed its own pattern. To Juliet its inhabitants seemed prisoners of the standards it implied, remote, and at the same time with a sense of stability and effortless self-confidence she found maddening. She was sure that bathing in the fountain didn't fit in.

"Where's your father?" she said. "Hadn't we better ask him first?"

Upsetting the ethos didn't matter to her, she was outside: but the children were in.

"He's out on the farm of course. *He* won't mind."

Martin said nothing.

"Oh well," Juliet got up off the grass.

"Come on." Harriet was swollen with an enormous excitement. She held magic in her hand. The garden was all hers, the house was empty, sleeping, through Juliet she could do what she liked. "It's so hot. You just have to turn up the tap. That's all."

"I don't know where the tap is."

"*We* do, we'll show you."

They ran away up the yew walk, round the rose bed, flittering up the stone steps on to the terrace with Juliet chasing after them.

"Here you are! Turn it up, turn it up! No!" The water drooped. "Not that way, the *other* way. Further! Further! Right as far as it'll go!"

The water shot with the full force of the main behind it, high into the air, falling beyond the fountain's basin, crashing on the flagstones with the noise of heavy rain. It was as if the sky had burst open and loosed down freedom.

"Catch me Juliet, catch me!"

"No catch *me*."

They dashed in and out of the water, opening their mouths to catch it as it fell. Wild staccato laughter floated over the wall and down the drive.

Gerald stopped dead at the corner of the terrace. His mouth open to shout with rage shut again. Except for two tiny triangles of brown satin tied with bows on her hips Juliet was naked. Her hair, parted in the middle, lay smooth close to her head, falling in twisting waves that glistened with water over her shoulders to touch her nipples. Pearly drops caught the sun and shone iridescent on her breasts. She was laughing. It was as if one of the naiads twined round the fountain had stepped down and come to life, leaving her sisters crude stone indeed.

Under his gaze she blushed, slowly, all over.

Harriet froze, transfixed by her father's anger. She hoped that if she kept quite still and held her breath she might somehow make herself invisible. Her father was large, sandy-coloured, fierce, but above all male and his displeasure was catastrophic.

It was Juliet he was looking at not her. The expression in his eyes was something Harriet had never seen before. Unnoticed she slipped away indoors. She wished Mummy was there. It was as if for a moment the world had slipped sideways.

Juliet bent down casually and restored the fountain to its normal gentle play.

"What about food?" Gerald said.

Harriet was almost afraid to come down to tea. Yet everything seemed quite ordinary. Juliet was dressed. Her father was talking about hay. Only Martin was gazing at Juliet in the same silly way the dogs gazed at Gerald.

2

It was the dead hour before dinner when the children were in bed and everyone else retired to their rooms to change for a civilised evening meal. There seemed no reason to Juliet why she should climb out of the perfectly clean green frock she had put on for tea into something else, but she was still too uncertain of what went in this house not to conform. Suppose Monica was about to give her the sack for playing in the fountain? It would be better not to add fuel to the flames. She took off the green frock and threw it on a chair.

The whole of this bedroom spoke to her, quite politely, about a life she neither liked nor understood, and she was beginning to wonder about the wisdom of coming here at all, where there was nothing to distract her from thinking about Oliver and what was going on between him and Lucy without her there to stop it. Oh well, if he didn't find out what a little creep Lucy was after six weeks alone with her and a Land-rover he wasn't worth having. She stared past the mirror to the heavy green trees outside, piqued all the same that for the first time in her life some male had not done exactly what she wanted.

She consoled herself with the idea that if the weather held she could get brown and digest *Beowulf* before going back to Oxford to trample on a chastened Oliver.

Dimly she was aware of doors opening and shutting and other people going downstairs. Not intending to give Gerald anything more to look at she hid herself in a kaftan.

On the other side of the passage Harriet spun out the bed-time conversation.

"Mummy don't go. Why is Juliet an au pair?"

"People at university all do holiday jobs."

"Why is she at university?"

"You ask her yourself tomorrow."

Harriet frowned.

"What's the matter, don't you like her, darling?"

"Oh it's not I don't *like* her."

"What, then? What's this all about?"

"Nothing. Really."

"Well then goodnight poppet," and Monica hurried downstairs to dish up.

"What have you been saying to the poor girl, Gerald?" she said as she came into the diningroom. Juliet's face was scarlet and Gerald wore the fat look he always did when he had scored a point. "Don't take any notice of him, Juliet, he's a terrible tease."

"I wasn't teasing. I was admiring her frock, she dresses very nicely. What are you giving us to eat tonight? We'll have a bottle of wine."

Juliet was keeping her eyes front across the highly polished table. Everything, from the bowl of sweet peas to the heavy silver cutlery, was double by reflection. Her feelings were double too. She was embarrassed at having been caught naked under the fountain, and simultaneously, acutely aware of Gerald's interest. She sidestepped by studying Monica, remote beyond the sweet peas.

"It's beef, darling," Monica said.

She shuts you out. I should never get to know her, if I tried for a thousand years, Juliet thought. Like the labradors: quite friendly, but exclusive to Gerald. There was a photograph on the piano in the drawingroom that had appeared in *Country Life* the year Monica came out. It showed a neat dark head and well-bred face above pearls and a round-necked sweater. Perhaps that sort of grooming for life had a deep freeze effect. Did she ever swear or say 'fuck'?

14

On the walls other well-bred ladies, past Mrs Websters in heavy gold frames, gazed blandly down.

Gerald filled Juliet's glass. She kept still, not wanting to be touched. The decanter, carrying the wine ruby-red in its belly and reflecting a hundred sharp points of light from its cut upper works, harmonised with the dark panelling and crimson velvet curtains. The wine itself, whether claret or burgundy Juliet didn't know, was better than anything she was used to. But there was nothing gay about the occasion. She would have preferred plonk by the camp fire on the way to Turkey.

"This is nice, Gerald." Monica turned to Juliet. "Were the children good this afternoon? Something upset Harriet. She took ages to settle. Then she wanted to know about the facts of life for about the hundredth time."

Under the table Gerald shifted his foot and firmly pressed Juliet's. Teasing, he waited to see what she would say.

"They were perfectly good, they were no trouble. Harriet wasn't a bit upset while they were with me." So he hadn't said anything. The old goat, that was his line, fun and games with the au pair. It was impossible to move her foot without a scuffle. She said sweetly to Monica, "Shall I clear? You've done all the hard work cooking."

"That's very kind. Everything's ready to bring in."

You're afraid of yourself, my girl, Gerald thought. He leant back in his chair and said to Monica, "What were you doing this afternoon? I saw you from the top of the stack, leaning over the gate talking to the dogs. Where were you off to?"

"I had tea with Rachel. Did you forget? I was trying to persuade Rex and Janus to come with us, but they were too lazy."

When Juliet came back into the room the atmosphere had changed. A domestic pall had fallen, Gerald offered only the politeness due to a stranger. Bored, she devoted herself to the strawberry shortcake. Food in this house was always worth attention.

She hoped the evening might flower into some sort of interest, some conversation, the tele, or even the mild pleasure of fending off unwanted admiration. But nothing of the sort happened. After dinner Gerald retired behind the pages of the *Farmer's Weekly*, apparently unaware that she was in the room. Monica busied herself with a piece of petit point, worked in fine wools. All the colours were muted. Sitting in their stuffed armchairs one each side of the marble fireplace husband and wife reminded Juliet of the toy on her mantelpiece at home that was supposed to tell the weather, but never did. They were stuck, like the two little people who would stay obstinately side by side, neither in nor out. Such lordliness mated to such static serenity made her want to burst a balloon or shout or put drawingpins on the chairs.

I suppose if you've been married nine years or whatever you're entitled not to speak, but if I'm a visitor it's rude, and as a gambit it's a ripe error.

Without lowering his paper Gerald said "I see Bomfords have brought out an interesting new green crop loader, Monica. I'd like to have a look at that."

"Why not darling? Oh Juliet, I expect you've already found out the children quarrel rather. Martin's not very good at standing up for himself. It's a bit hard being the youngest, really."

The flesh turned weary on Juliet's bones. "They seem fine to me. I think I'll go up to bed if that's all right."

"I'm afraid you won't find anything much to read in your room. Try the library if you want a book. Gerald uses it as his office, but you won't mind Juliet going in to get one, will you darling?"

"As many as she likes."

His voice was friendly, but he didn't look up.

Monica's needle went up and down and in and out between the threads of her canvas. Gerald's hands holding the paper came together as he considered Juliet's back view, then stretched again. As the door shut Monica raised her eyes from her embroidery. "She seems a nice enough child," she said.

Juliet's father kept an antiquarian bookshop, and from all he'd told her about what the word 'library' could mean her expectations were low: stuffed heads and crossed guns, old magazines in heaps, a few shelves of secondrate Victorian novels. On opening the door she had a shock of pleasure and surprise. The library had been designed for the use of a scholar and a gentleman when the house was built, and leatherbound books lined the oblong room from floor to moulded ceiling. Sometime in the nineteenth century projecting cases had been added, dividing the two long walls into bays. Outside the window at the far end the fountain played and the falling water kept the light in the room alive.

On a pedestal to the right of the window a curly haired bust of Virgil, carved about 1820, surveyed the scene with blind eyes. In the bay to the left Gerald had installed his desk, a green metal filing cabinet, and one expanding bookcase full of technical works. A farming calendar hung from a drawingpin stuck in the shelving. Stuffed in among the agricultural books were a few thrillers in paperback.

Juliet thought: 'He doesn't deserve to own this.'

There were no gay new paper jackets and the few clothbound volumes on the shelves had faded and looked stale. Except for Gerald's rough encampment nothing was newer than 1900.

But cheek by jowl with ancient rubbish was all Lit. Hum. and all Eng. Lit. in beautiful editions. Her hand went straight to a first edition of *Don Juan*, and for a moment she was back 150 years in time. Along with the smell of old paper and old leather the feel of the past itself came out of the pages. This book had arrived hot from the press, fraught with moral danger. Keats had written it off as 'Lord Byron's last flash poem'. The public, less discriminating, had been wildly excited. What had the people living here thought? How had

17

they felt when they undid the parcel? Byron had been the arch hippy of his day. No current hippy's work would ever nest on these shelves.

To see whether anyone would notice the gap she took *Don Juan* up to bed.

She was thinking as she mounted the curve of the stairs 'I could never live here. The house doesn't let you impinge. It may be all right for the family, they've been conditioned from birth, but the past has a say in every step you make. It would be like trying to live in the V and A.' It didn't matter how much chaos she made in her bedroom it still preserved its faultless good taste, remorselessly comfortable down to the envelopes and paper on the writing table and biscuits in a box by her bed. Tempted by the joke of such an outsider as herself using the headed paper, she sat down to write a letter.

"Dear Oliver——". She stared out of the window. Her pen dropped on to the paper and executed a little doodle. Seeing the sheet was ruined she crumpled it up, threw it in the wastepaper basket and started again. In the end she gave up and went to have a bath.

Monica had said "I hope you don't mind using the children's bathroom. It is nearer your room. Then Gerald's mother likes to have one to herself when she comes."

At first this had seemed amusing; the bathroom was a complete Victorian survival. The bath had brass taps and mahogany panelling, with two steps up, orange-brown de Morgan tiles protected the wall behind. Even the original embossed wallpaper, beige, its surface shiny with a thick brownish varnish, had never been changed. But tonight it struck her as sick, a hang-up. 'The man has embalmed his childhood in his grandfather's bathroom,' she thought, lowering herself into the water.

What an evening. Steam rose enveloping her in a thick mist. Damn Oliver. Landing her in this mausoleum. D.V. the Landrover conked. Miles from nowhere, and Lucy did her helpless female act, in pouring rain or boiling sun, it didn't much matter which. Then he'd see what he'd saddled himself with.

In spite of her deliberate plan that Oliver should be sickened of Lucy by having her stuffed up his nose, at this moment Juliet thought what a pity it was they couldn't change places. Lucy would fit in here too well for words. She'd lap up Gerald and his moribund stately home and love every minute of them both. They'd give her something to talk about for the whole term. "She'd suit the old lech down to the ground," she told the tap. "It's a sandy man, too pink like they always are."

To top up the bath she turned the tap on with her foot; an orange plastic fish fell out of the rack into the water. How odd it was to be an au pair, it was precisely what one was not; like using the children's not the visitors' bathroom. Even Mrs Barden who came daily from the village and was a nice old thing wouldn't accept her, either as Family, or Help, and made it quite plain she thought an au pair a mistake.

For a moment Juliet was angry that one small family should have so much and do so little with it, keeping up worn out traditions, believing themselves superior to the rest of mankind simply because they'd been born to landed property. The house rattled round them as if they'd shrunk.

Downstairs a door opened. Gerald and Monica's voices floated up. Footsteps, unmistakeably Gerald's, padded down the passage and switched off the light outside the bathroom door. Why? He knew she was still in there. It was a sexual gesture, as physical as the pressure of his foot under the table.

A bedroom door opened and shut. The bath was getting cold; the loneliness was too great for her to get out.

The two chief objects in Monica's bedroom were an eighteenth century rosewood dressingtable with an oval mirror, and a large fourposter bed. Monica was already in the bed. She was watching Gerald brushing his hair with her hairbrush. He was stark naked. His arms were brown gloves to just above the elbow, his head and neck made a helmet ending in a sharp brown V on his chest. The rest of his body was very white, and except for his bush and the tufts of hair under his arms, smooth. He was like a priapic figure on a vase.

"Don't be too unkind to Rachel," she said, suddenly sorry for her because she wasn't going to see Gerald naked again.

"My God women are immoral. What a time to choose to talk about Rachel." He drew the curtains of the bed to shut out surplus light. "There's a lot to be said for fourposters, they show a proper respect for the art of lovemaking."

The bed-curtains made a room within a room. Outside, harts fled across a tapestry landscape; inside, cherry coloured silk diffused a pink glow. The original hangings had disintegrated in Gerald's mother's reign and she had substituted floral chintz, but when Gerald moved her to the dower house he made her take her curtains with her. He replaced them with exact replicas of a Stuart design, specially woven in honour of his marriage to Monica. He had chosen Monica carefully, wedded her a virgin, and set her apart to be loved above everything. He regarded her as his property; but as his wife she was lifted into a world of ancestral rites and privileges no mistress would ever be allowed to enter. She was almost an extension of himself. The setting had to be worthy.

From the first Gerald was continuously unfaithful, yet Monica was happy and perfectly content. She never stopped to analyse what it was he gave her in addition to physical passion that made her marriage so satisfying and his infidelities of no account. She only knew that he had come into her life a god-like Young Lochinvar and carried her off. She was not given to analysis, and in any case where was the need?

Gerald lay with his head on her breast. She ran her fingers through his hair. She had such complete fulfilment she didn't grudge the leftover attention his mistresses had from him. Out of her infinite wealth she could spare it. Poor sad women, they

20

couldn't be expected to understand how unimportant they were. It was just as well they didn't know that Gerald brought his affairs to her as the dogs brought their bones.

"Poor Rachel," she said.

"Yes, tell me now, what did she want?"

"She's afraid you're bored."

"So I am."

"What did you see in her? She's got terrible legs. You're usually fussy about legs."

"I don't know; her breasts. She's got extraordinary large brown areolas and fat nipples. I've never seen anything quite like them. And she was sex-starved. It was quite something. Her husband's too fat and drinks too much, he can't get a rise more than once a month. He makes a note of the date in his diary and keeps pegging away hoping one day he'll produce a child."

"What a ghastly fate. Why on earth did she marry him I wonder?"

"Money. She'd never stand being poor."

"Poor thing. But what a fool. What a dreadful house it is, Gerald. I don't know why those sort of people want to live in the country. They don't begin to understand what it's about. They just bring their little bit of suburbia with them. She'd be much happier in Haywards Heath. I suppose now we shall have to have them to dinner."

"God forbid."

"You make it very awkward for me. What *did* go on this afternoon when I was out? I saw you looking at Juliet. You were teasing. What was the matter with Harriet?"

"One of them turned up the fountain and they were prancing underneath in their pants. I didn't tick them off because Juliet was supposed to be in charge. But Harriet knew quite well she's been naughty."

"Gerald you're fibbing."

"Well, Juliet was in her pants too."

"Look, Gerald. Not the au pair, not under you own roof, not the children's companion. It's too much. You might as well go for Mrs Barden's Betty."

"You know I'd never do that," he said stuffily. "I never have anything to do with that sort of girl. I couldn't sleep with a girl I wouldn't take out to dinner."

"Oh Gerald, really."

"What's the matter?"

"Sometimes you're too good to be true. Sometimes I don't understand you at all."

"You're the only person who does."

"Well, not Juliet, please."

"Have you noticed," he said, "She's got the most remarkable hair. She's almost a redhead. I've never had a redhead." His voice was hushed.

"Redhead? You could imagine a brunette into a redhead, but Gerald, darling, not by the wildest stretch of the imagination a blonde like Juliet."

"I would have said sort of auburn lights. Redgold. Very unusual." With his free hand he stretched round the hangings to turn out the light. Then he kissed her gently.

3

Inside, the house was waiting for life to start, silent except for the tick of the grandfather clock in the hall. Outside, the day had already dawned cloudless behind the early morning haze. Thick dew lay on the lawn like frost.

Martin woke up first. No one stirred. In the other bed Harriet was still fast asleep. He crept out, tiptoed along the passage to Juliet's room and softly turned the handle; she was asleep too. Gently, so as not to disturb her, he lifted up the bedclothes and slid in beside her. His cold feet and stiff little legs touching hers woke her up. She looked at his solemn face, smiled, turned over and went to sleep again. For a long time he sat bolt upright watching her breathe: how long her eyelashes were, how soft her pink cheeks looked. At last chilliness got the better of his awe and he wriggled cautiously under the bedclothes. In her sleep she put an arm around him and tucked him against her breasts. Utterly happy he went to sleep too. Left unfastened, the door opened quietly on to the empty passage.

Neither of them woke again till the sun was streaming in and breakfast smells were drifting on the air. To make Martin get up Juliet tickled him, and in the wild fight that followed the bedclothes hurtled off the bed on to the floor till the mattress was bare and he fled in helpless laughter, holding up his pyjama trousers with one hand.

Downstairs the others were already half way through breakfast.

"*We've* been working," Harriet said smugly. "I've been out with Daddy. Doing the tomatoes. Lazybones. *I* know where

23

you were."

"You're not to say."

"If it's private you shouldn't've left the door open."

"Don't tease, Harriet," Monica said. "If Martin's a nuisance Juliet'll say. Your Granny's coming next week. You'd better practise being good."

"Goody," both children said together, thinking of the treats to be extracted. "Will she be here for the fête?"

"Yes. So she says. She wants to come on Monday, Gerald. Can you meet her, or shall I?"

"Need we decide now?"

"You know she'll be put out if she doesn't know which of us to expect. Why don't you two children go fishing this morning? I've got nothing for the poor cats."

Mrs Webster senior had long since removed from the Dower House to a hotel on the front at Eastbourne, where the necessity never arose even to wash up a teacup. As Gerald knew perfectly well, all that had ever interested her about the village was the position she held there, and this she had lost to Monica: the dower house was an empty gift, from a smiling victor, gall and wormwood wrapped up as a favour. Mrs Webster enjoyed more physical comfort in her present style of life and endless drama was to be had out of the sudden visits she made to the Hall.

Gerald frowned. As soon as Juliet and the children left the room he said, "Last time it was lambing, this time it's hay-making. She always manages to descend at the vital wrong moment."

"I know darling. I'll take her off you all I can." Monica looked at him anxiously. He was worrying about himself, the farming was camouflage. His mother always upset him. Her impact even from a distance was disastrous. "If you like I'll go and meet her. Juliet'll be here, after all."

Gerald left his mother's letter lying on the table between them.

"If the children are going fishing Juliet can help me with the tomatoes," he said.

The greenhouse was beyond the stable yard, extending all along the outside of the south wall of the vegetable garden. It had been built in 1850 to house exotica, and the semi-tropical tomato plants were quite at home. The hot air was thick with their acrid smell. Row on long row the plants made a strong jungle growth, their leaves curling, their stems prickling with little stiff hairs; here and there, at the extremities, clusters of pale yellow flowers were beginning to unfurl, each blossom nursing a tiny embryo tomato. Green plastic netting against the glass gave protection from scorching, but down below among the plants it was difficult to breathe, even with the door and all the ventilation open. Stepping inside the greenhouse was to step into a pocket of foreign atmosphere.

"What you do is to pinch out the side shoots between the leaves and the stem. Look, like this. Start on this one."

Gerald was soothed by the sight of Juliet among the green leaves. All her movements were fluid and full of sensual delicacy, her fingers breaking off the shoots were slow; she was wearing a pale green dress that barely covered her bottom, and the hairy tomato stalks made her long smooth brown legs look smoother than ever.

What was more unusual in someone so decorative, she was easy to be with. She made no demands.

Little by little her rhythm had a hypnotic effect and his tension drained away.

Juliet was thinking about Martin, going over in her mind the novel sensation of holding him asleep in her arms. His little body had been taut and hard, not soft as she had imagined.

The leaves of the tomatoes ran into each other and made a screen. She was on one side, Gerald on the other. He had gone several plants ahead and his voice took her by surprise.

"I'll just finish this one off for you, then we can start level pegging."

But soon she was left behind again and she made a looping progress down the row, like a caterpillar, the distance between them opening and shutting. To her surprise she found the tomato plants very restful. They were busy growing away in an uncomplicated vegetable manner and the heat inside the greenhouse was soporific. She and Gerald were both absorbed into their process of growth. How odd. Watching him working she decided his wolf persona was a front. What weakness was it a cover up for? She wondered what he was really like behind that leching mask, but when she thought, in some curious way he and Martin merged.

From the other side of the green barrier Gerald, amused at her absent face, finding her young detachment moving, was content with the intimate silence, comfortably aware that it would be a tactical error to press.

They were interrupted by a car hooting from the drive.

"Damn," Gerald said, "I'd better go."

He didn't come back, the greenhouse was quite simply too hot. It occurred to Juliet she was here to look after children, not tomatoes. She saw them from halfway across the field. They were standing motionless on the edge of the pond, their rods parallel. Oliver and Lucy were a long way away. Surrounded by the burgeoning countryside, where nothing was hurrying, all trace of responsibility dropped from her. Only her immediate sensations impinged. The feel of sun on her skin, long dry grasses brushing her leg, tiny insects moving, birds flashing across the sky, stretched to infinity.

Under the oak tree the pond was in deep shadow. She could see no reflections in the black opaque water. The fish were biting and bright little roach were scattered like splinters of glass behind Martin on the bank in the sun.

Without looking round Harriet said "Have you finished, then?"

"No. Your father had to go off somewhere."

"Oh. If you like you can have a turn with my rod. It's easy.

26

See? When the float goes under you wait a sec and then pull. If you don't like taking the fish off the hook Martin will do it for you. Try. Really, I mean it."

Juliet took the rod. "I've done this before," she said, "in the sea. It's different but the same."

"There," Hariet said. "Martin's got one."

The red and white float bobbed once, and again, and then dived. The line stretched tight, Martin pulled, and a fish flew jacknifing over their heads. Absorbed, Martin extricated the hook and rebaited it in silence. The only thing that appeared of any importance to Juliet was to experience the beautiful manoeuvre herself.

Harriet disappeared, sidling round the barn where the cow parsley grew taller than her waist; its strong smell meant summer.

All the morning she had been cross, because it was her province to help her father in the greenhouse, not Juliet's. He was unfair. She let the pollen brush off on to her arm. It had magic properties that might come in useful. She went to find him, thinking he was bound to come back to finish off the tomatoes. But the greenhouse was deserted.

Gerald slammed the door of the white car shut and strode into the house. "Bitch," he said under his breath, "bitch."

It outraged his sense of decency that Rachel should turn up uninvited and make a scene in his drive.

And besides, no woman had the right to ask a man whether he loved her, it implied he didn't know the rules. Gerald prided himself on not cheating, he had made it quite clear from the beginning that there was no question of love.

And what impertinence to cast Juliet in his teeth, just because she had nice legs! He'd never laid a finger on the girl. "Watch it," Rachel had said, "she's the sort men go overboard for. I hope you suffer."

What did Rachel know about men? Bitch!

He shouted inside the hall "Monica! I'll be in the library."

Monica found him frowning at the top of his desk while putting a letter into an envelope.

"Your tea," she said. "What on earth's the matter? Who was that car screeching up the drive?"

"That was Rachel."

"Ah I *see*."

"Bloody ill-bred. She was making such a noise I had to get into the car and turn up the windows."

"Perhaps she's unhappy. Perhaps she's fond of you, poor woman."

"Don't you believe it. Nothing but sex and then she short-changed me. Making out she had something to give when she is nothing but a great hole. She's a sexual con."

"Oh dear."

"She wears porno pants—you know, black lace with a pink velvet heart stuck over the bush—under that assets you could only rate banal, and when I get there she expects me to do it all."

They were both utterly serious. Monica afforded the subject the same attention as she would have the milk yield of Gerald's cows.

"How odd darling. She looks so sultry. I wouldn't have expected her to be one of those limp women. She's not frigid, surely Gerald?"

"Quite the opposite. I wouldn't have minded if she'd been frigid, that's a challenge. She was dying for it. She's greedy, that's the trouble with her. She just lay like a log and took it all in. She didn't *move*."

"How *awful* for you."

"And she thinks herself worth serious attention! It's an insult to a man. She can go and walk the streets. I'm not interested in lust." For the first time he noticed the cup in front of him. "This tea's cold." He pushed it away. A queer

28

mixed expression came over his face.

"Ah, never mind. Poor darling. But you're pleased, really, aren't you, that there's been a scene?"

"Well, yes, of course. At least I don't have to go through the tiresome routine of dropping her kindly."

Monica stared out into the sunshine at the fountain playing rainbow colours. "We shan't have to have them to dinner now, that's one relief. They're such bores. That's one woman I don't mind not being able to meet."

Gerald said "I've written to Mother. I've told her I'll meet her train, but if she misses it or changes her mind at the last minute she'll have to order a taxi."

"Why provoke her, darling?"

"I'm not. Believe me, she'll like it. It's the kind of ping-pong she understands," and talking about his mother put a savage edge on his voice.

Walking past the window Harriet paused, and passed slowly on.

"What's that child up to now I wonder?" Monica said. "She's looking for you in the most obvious unobvious way."

She wished Rachel had been less inept because this was just the wrong moment for Gerald to be at an emotional loose end.

Martin and Juliet were late for lunch. They came in with half a bucketful of fish and their radiant happiness so imposed itself, holding everyone in its ambience, that Monica couldn't be cross. Only Harriet looked sideways and said "Can't you tell the time?"

4

While Gerald had been striding back to the house muttering 'bitch,' Mrs Barden was saying to Monica in the kitchen:

"I think you ought to know, Madam, Miss Juliet keeps the Pill on her dressing-table." She had been going to add 'I don't think you should keep her in the house.' Instead, feeling the reproof in Monica's face, she said:

"Well, it was there for all the world to see."

I must tell her to put them away, Monica thought. In case the children think they're sweeties. Martin has been in Juliet's room already. She couldn't think how to say this to Juliet. The problem grew at once to enormous proportions till it stuck in her throat.

I suppose it would be too much to expect innocence in a girl as pretty as that, in these days, and at a university. But innocent was what Juliet's face was, across the lunch table, as untroubled as Martin's.

"You don't need the car this afternoon do you Gerald?" she said, pushing the whole subject on one side.

"God forbid."

"Can we come? Please."

"No. I've got too much to do getting ready for your Granny. I'll be in a hurry."

"But we want ice creams."

"Don't be annoying, children. If you're good we'll play hide and seek," Gerald said.

The game started from the terrace, with the traditional ceremony of *eeni-meeni-mini-mo*.

"o-u-t spells out, so out you must go. I'm He," Gerald said firmly. "The fountain's home, if you have one foot touching the rim you're safe. Now run along all of you and look sharp because I count fast. You've got to a hundred. One, two, three—"

"No Martin, you're not to come with me. Find your own hiding place," Harriet said.

Juliet took him by the hand.

"Fifty-one, fifty-two . . ." Gerald counted. "A hundred. Coming!"

Silence fell over the garden as Gerald, from his vantage point on the terrace, took stock of the position. Harriet was invisible. She had gone to ground among the azaleas and other flowering shrubs that grew along the garden wall beyond the big elm to the left of the doorway on to the drive. Martin had hidden in full view, behind the sundial in the middle of the rose garden below the terrace. He was standing rigid, with his eyes shut. Juliet had flattened herself into the deep shadow in the angle between the terrace wall and the stone steps, mobile, ready to take off in the opposite direction to any Gerald might choose. He didn't see her partly because he didn't expect her to be there.

Martin rocked on his feet. "I see you," Gerald shouted, advancing down the steps. Behind his back Harriet raced for home. Juliet rose out of her corner.

"Ha! There's another one."

"Run, Martin," she said and sprinted round the edge of the terrace, up the bank, behind Harriet. Gerald ran back up the steps to head her off.

Martin followed him on to the terrace but made no effort to be safe. "No you mustn't, no you mustn't," he was shouting, hopping up and down in agony. "Don't, don't," he said as Gerald blocked Juliet's access to home.

Hunter and hunted faced each other, panting, dodging,

round the elm tree. Then Juliet swerved through the orchard doorway out of sight on to the drive.

"Got you!" Gerald said, pinning her arms.

His eyes were blazing. She felt his kiss in her vitals. 'No!' flashed through her head.

"Juliet's caught, Juliet's He," he shouted, letting her go and running back towards the open door. "You must count from where you are, Juliet. Come on now, children!"

The kiss had been so swift Juliet wondered for a second if there had been one at all. But when she looked at Gerald as he disappeared through the doorway on to the terrace the blood surged through her body. So it had happened.—What of it?— She put her hands over her face and began to count aloud, "One, two—"

Gerald was soon home. He stood triumphantly by the fountain, one foot on the rim, watching her chase the children.

Martin ran drunkenly, swaying from side to side, helpless with laughter, looking backwards over his shoulder.

"You're not trying," Juliet said. "Run, run, or I'll catch you." Unable to help herself, she swept him up in her arms. "Now you're He."

Harriet stood on the outside. She'd given up trying to get home. In her mind the game of hide and seek had become a duel betwen her father and Juliet, with Martin sucked into the middle, a helpless victim.

"I don't like this game," she said.

"Harriet needs to be He. That's what it is. You catch her, Martin," Gerald said.

But Martin caught Gerald, and then Gerald chasing Harriet down the yew walk, caught her and picked her up and carried her back on his shoulders, making her forget her unhappiness.

"I'm exhausted," he said. "You run too fast," and the game was over.

Monica had opened the front door with her head full of Mrs Webster at the very moment when Gerald caught Juliet. In the widening bar of sunshine they danced up and down in front of her eyes like a cloud of motes in a sunbeam. By the time she could see straight Gerald was already running towards the terrace shouting to the children and Juliet was standing with her hands over her eyes, counting in a loud voice. Was it a kiss or wasn't it? Monica shut the door again and stood in the hall feeling sick. This was the first time she had actually seen Gerald kissing a very pretty girl and she was seized by uncontrollable jealousy. It was a *coup de foudre*. Falling in love with Gerald had been like that too, changing her life in a flash.

But this change was in the opposite direction, and it took her life out of her hands.

She couldn't think. Her mind was filled by disjointed images: Gerald's hands on Juliet's arms; their two heads together, Gerald shouting, all coming together in a vision of livid, shimmering, copulating bodies. The words 'Juliet keeps the Pill on her dressingtable' ran like tickertape through her head.

'I asked him not to.'

Her feelings were so savage she was frightened, and told herself she had imagined the kiss.

'If you catch someone at hide and seek you often bump into them; that's all it was.'

'Anyway it's no use getting excited. If Gerald was kissing Juliet he'll tell me about it in bed tonight.'

'I can always send her away.'

But her reasonable remarks were sexually unconvincing, just a film of words as far as her emotions were concerned.

Her hand was hurting her. 'What has happened to me?' she thought, 'I'm holding on to the car key as if life depended on it.'

Long practice in self-control compelled her to open the front door again, get into the car, ignore the shouts of laughter, drive off, and complete her shopping without allowing the raging tumult inside her to show. She even remembered to buy ice creams for the children and make sure that it was properly wrapped in thick newspaper so as not to melt on the way home.

That night, behind the tapestry bed-hangings, where the springing harts forever escaped the hunter, Gerald made love to Monica with extra tenderness. Monica understood his mute appeal for comfort and she responded, comforted herself. 'He needs me just the same,' she thought, and was calmed and reassured. Nothing was said.

5

Sunday came as a surprise to Juliet. She had no idea such archaic practices still existed. There was no lie-in. Monica called her at the same time as on a weekday.

"The service here is at nine," she said, "so people can go out for the day afterwards if they want to. I've told Martin he can wear his blue linen shorts and white shirt. If he can't find it, his tie's in the top drawer. And you might just make sure Harriet doesn't forget to put on socks."

Juliet had had no intention of going herself, but she was involved before she knew what was happening.

Martin said "You can sit next me in church." He had wetted his hair and plastered it flat with a hairbrush. Both children looked unnaturally clean and virtuous.

"I'm afraid I haven't got a hat."

"Don't you go to church?" Harriet sounded shocked.

"No one minds about hats," Monica said quickly, "but I think it's polite to be reasonably tidy."

Juliet realised this was levelled at her bare legs.

She didn't want to disappoint Martin, besides, she was moved by the spirit of pure research; she went with the tide, first veiling her legs in tights.

When Gerald came down to breakfast his face above his Sunday suit was wearing the smooth look Monica recognised as belonging to the beginning of a new love affair, and her precarious equilibrium collapsed.

"If you had a headache Mummy would you go to church?" Harriet said staring.

"I've not got one, so it doesn't come in."

"No, but would you?"

"It depends how bad the headache was. But I haven't, and I know quite well you haven't either. If you don't look what you're doing you'll spill egg down your clean frock."

The church was only half a mile away but they went by car, Monica in front, carrying gloves and an ivory-backed prayer book, Juliet with the children behind. Harriet and Martin had their own prayer books too, and Juliet felt alien all over again, and for a moment embarrassed.

Inside the church the verger ushered them up the aisle to where the squires of the village had sat for generations, and held open the pew door. The church had escaped the ravages of nineteenth century restoration and still possessed its black oak box pews. Gerald motioned Juliet to go in first, then Harriet, followed by Martin, Monica and himself. The verger shut them in.

Juliet couldn't see the rest of the congregation. The squire's pew was on the left hand side, right in front and she was up against the wall. Her view was limited to the pulpit, two vases of blue delphiniums flanking the altar, and the roof overhead where parallel beams made a neat pattern. On the wall above her head a plaque commemorated the dead. 'Sacred to the memory of Martin Webster who fell at Dunkirk 2nd May 1940 aetat 26. He died in the service of his country. Their name liveth for ever more.' She worked out from this that Gerald couldn't be younger than 32, and was unlikely to be more than 37. The church bell was tolling on a single note now. Gerald's face along the pew to her right wore a strange remote look in keeping with the carved heads at the pew ends. He was almost part of the church itself. Monica's face was hidden in her hands, Juliet could see nothing but her shining dark hair. Beside her, Harriet and Martin were shuffling into their seats, settling themselves down and smoothing their clothes as children do when some known ritual is about to begin.

38

The bell hesitated, rang twice, there was a short silence. Then the organ began to play, the choir, a mixed assortment of men, women and boys, trooped in, and the parson entered and faced the congregation.

He was an old man, white, Juliet thought, like a fish. His hair was white, his face was a wrinkled dirty white, above his white surplice his hands clasping the pulpit edge were white too. Out of his gills came totally unintelligible gibberish. Years of saying morning prayer had led him to play with the words and his voice to give himself variety, putting his accents now here now there with no regard to the sense, to make a pattern of sounds. His diction was impaired beyond recall.

Juliet could only follow by referring to the prayer book in front of her. She thought 'How beautiful the words are'—"*In His hands are all the corners of the earth and the strength of the hills is His also.*"

But the whole apparatus of the service left her unmoved. She couldn't dissociate from Fish-face mouthing the language, or from the stale smell of hassock and wood and stone. She felt like some anthropological field worker attending a primitive tribal rite.

"*Requisite and necessary, as well for the body as the soul.*" 'What do these people mean by all this?'

Now everyone was murmuring through their fingers in a communal groan full of whispers: "*We have done those things we ought not to have done, and there is no health in us . . .*"

Harriet nudged Martin and turned to the back of her prayer book, disclosing several sheets of blank paper carefully folded to size. Martin extricated a pencil from his trouser pocket and drew out the squares for noughts and crosses.

'This is a farce,' Juliet thought. Martin's solemn face above his pale blue tie made her cross. Why dress children up in ties on a marvellous fine day and bring them here for this?

But the children would have disliked being left behind.

39

Owing to a series of games that belonged to definite parts of the service they were not bored, and they both enjoyed the singing. Habit might one day lead them to acceptance like Monica's, or even devotion such as Gerald's.

An inkling of this and that it was part of something she would never understand and didn't belong to came to Juliet and made her crosser still.

Monica had been brought up to believe in the Christian faith and going to church as part of that station in life to which God had been pleased to call her. She came out of the service every Sunday feeling vaguely better, but the spiritual fulfilment she would have liked to experience eluded her. Today she couldn't concentrate at all. When she put down her gloves and knelt beside Gerald to pray all she could think about was what had happened between him and Juliet.

'If only I had seen clearly, if I knew he'd kissed her, I could have had it out with him.' Behind her laced fingers she tried to visualise what had actually taken place, and failed. All she saw was the door opening then a bar of sunlight striped across her mind blurred everything.

To her left the children were quiet and occupied, to her right Gerald was already absent from her. 'How I envy him,' Monica thought. 'And he's not the one in need. It's not him that's in trouble.'

Only Gerald was following every word of the service, praying in the hopes of placating God in advance for the sin he knew he was about to commit, acknowledging to Him that he meant to have Juliet. He was praying with the utmost sincerity, feeling himself to be in the presence of both his God and his ancestors. When he knelt down on the spot where his forbears had knelt for two and a half centuries and opened the prayer book used by his grandfather and great-grandfather before him, the age old meaning of the ritual shone clear, no matter what the shortcomings of the current incumbent, and he achieved the genuine spiritual exaltation denied to Monica.

40

He made no reservations. He wanted to be good and knew he sinned. He knew he was going to sin again, and that he couldn't help it. He would have understood waiting barefoot at Canossa in order to wipe out the past yet go on as before. But he believed, quite simply, that if he opened his heart and confessed God would understand and forgive him.

"We have erred and strayed from Thy ways like lost sheep ... there is no health in us."

'No. None,' Monica thought.

'But if it did happen, does it really matter anyway? Look at all Gerald's other women, they mean nothing.

'Ah, but he's always talked about them. He's said nothing about Juliet, not since about her hair.

'Perhaps there's nothing to say?'

Then Monica saw quite plainly Gerald's face as it had been at breakfast. If there was nothing yet there soon would be. 'If he doesn't tell me then everything is different and I don't understand any more.'

"Unto whom I sware in my wrath: that they should not enter into my rest," she sang.

'Why not simply send Juliet away and be done with the whole thing? But suppose there's nothing in it?' The extreme indelicacy of speaking to Juliet in such terms, as if she was an old-fashioned servant girl—and particularly if she was innocent—made Monica blush. She couldn't bring herself to inflict such an indignity on either Juliet or herself. 'How can I say to Juliet "I'm afraid you'll have to go, because I can't trust my husband to behave himself?" ' She could see Juliet's eyebrows, raised in mild contempt.

Besides, how to explain to Gerald? Monica could feel his body beside her, they were actually touching, but removed in his devotions he might have been light years away. The very nature of her marriage with him, that had been up till now a cause of pride and conscious superiority, tied her hands. She could hear his voice 'You're the only woman in the world who

41

wouldn't make a fuss. There's nothing I can't tell you.' I can't ask him. What would he think of me? It would be the end of trust between us. I'll have to wait and see. In any case Juliet will go away.

She got to her feet realising she had not heard one word of the lesson. *"We praise thee, O God:"* she was singing, but her evil train of thought refused to leave her alone.

Be reasonable. Gerald's said nothing so it's probably all imagination. It's not like him to kiss Juliet while he's playing with his children. It would be against all his principles.

So if he did? Then Juliet isn't the same as the others.

"When Thou tookest upon Thee to deliver man: Thou didst not abhor the Virgin's womb."

Monica was seized by a spasm of anger in her vagina against Gerald for tying her in an emotional contract that was so hard to bear. 'I won't bear it, I'll have it out with him.'

But a cold inner voice said 'Suppose he lies? Where are you then? Suppose he has already lied?' The very stone slabs beneath the hassock where she knelt seemed to Monica to shift and quake.

"Lord have mercy upon us," indeed. She put her whole heart into the Lord's Prayer.

Over and over again she asked, trying to get rid of her blinding fear, 'Please God, help me, what shall I do?'

"O God, make clean our hearts within us." I understand that, she thought. I must trust. There's nothing else.

Now everyone was singing *"Praise my soul the King of Heaven,"* with the special vigour the final hymn always inspires, looking out their offerings, putting ready their gloves. The plate came round and Martin had to be helped to find his sixpence.

When Monica got up off her knees to file out of church she had succeeded to some extent in drawing a veil over her pain and leaving her problem behind, pending, in God's lap.

Gerald held the pew door open for her feeling purged and

refreshed as he did every Sunday.

Outside the porch in the sunshine Martin asked Juliet "Which is your favourite hymn? We didn't have mine today, it's Onward Christian Soldiers."

"Juliet's a heathen," Gerald said, "she hasn't got a favourite hymn."

Not sure whether his father was teasing or if he really meant it, Martin took her hand and held it tight.

"The one at the end," Juliet said, and wondered how Gerald had guessed.

"Oh, you mean 'Praise him, praise him,' " said Martin, "why?"

6

Juliet lay on the hot terrace in the sun, reading the colour supplement, enjoying the gin and tonic put into her hand, while the stiffness of church seeped out of her system. She was vaguely aware of unusual fuss over lunch somewhere in the background, but not being called on to take part, let it flow over her head in silence.

Meanwhile for Monica Sunday morning was being ruined by the presence of a cuckoo in the nest. Usually this was a serene moment in her week, formal but intimate, and much looked forward to, when, by carefully juggling with drinks, roast beef and fruit pie, she created a feeling of leisure and the presence of servants in the background. When friends came round after church, that fitted in. But Juliet did not. Lying there reading, contributing no polite conversation, accepting ministrations as a matter of course, she turned the illusion inside out and made Monica herself feel like a servant. Plain instead of pretty, and no temptation to Gerald, Juliet would still have been in the way.

'I must have been mad,' Monica thought. 'Never again.'

Up in her room after lunch Juliet peeled off her tights. The cool air on her legs was a positive pleasure and made her feel more normal. The children were being taken out to bathe and she listened with relief to the car as it started up below her window and shot off down the drive. Now the whole place was hers in peace and she could relax. By leaning on the window-sill she could see the formal gardens away to her left, stretching empty, a living green against the hay-coloured park. The only sound was the persistent fountain splashing into its basin.

'If I could have this without any of them I'd never want to leave,' she thought, and envied Harriet for belonging here by right. Then she thought no, even in this walk of life the female is pushed. Sooner or later Harriet would have to go. It was Martin who was secure, tied here, whether he wanted it or not.

The local bus timetable, pressed on her by Monica, filled her with languor, conjuring up dust and the hot countryside smelt through petrol. In imagination she was already on her way down between dark yew walls to the hidden oasis above the ha-ha. She put on her bikini and picked up *Beowulf* from the blotter. The book was broken backed, the text annotated and underlined in ink by previous owners; a set book, it had passed and repassed through Blackwells. It was out of key both with her mood and setting. She took it with her as a talisman, to remind her that she didn't in fact belong here.

At the end of the yew walk the turf was like velvet and faintly moist, even in the sun. Juliet lay on her back and closed her eyes while *Beowulf*, open beside her, buckled in the heat.

In her leaf-brown bikini, asleep under the peacock, Juliet looked to Gerald as if earth and yews between them had given birth to her for his special benefit.

Almost loth to disturb her, he put his hand lightly on her breast.

"Oliver," she said, opening her eyes, ready to dissolve into his arms without further words. She didn't adjust at once to the sight of Gerald's face above her: blue eyes instead of brown, and lines of experience and suppressed anxiety. When she did, it was an erotic shock to find she wanted him inside her just as much as if it had been Oliver. "I thought you'd gone out."

"No. I had accounts to do. I saw you pass my window and guessed you'd be here. D'you mind if I come and interrupt you? Were you asleep?"

46

"I'm awake now," she said with an effort, still shocked that she could want both men at the same time. She didn't know her own body. It had turned traitor. She wasn't even seeing Gerald as pink. His gaze embarrassed her. She wouldn't have minded if he had tried to undress her, or if she had been stark naked already, but the look in his eyes made her feel stripped, exposed to a sort of mental voyeurism. It seemed to her her desire shouted to the four winds. Nothing in her life so far had prepared her for this unbridled sensuality. She rolled over on to her front.

Frightened by her own response, she protected herself with rudeness. "Well, which gambit are you playing? The unhappy childhood one?"

"I think I'd better go back to my accounts and let you sleep."

"All right. Do."

The open pages of *Beowulf* caught Gerald's eye.

"What a way to treat a book. I hope you won't do that with my first edition Byron."

Furious at being in the wrong Juliet blushed all over. Gerald watched, entranced, as the pink spread down her back, changing her honey-coloured skin. Then he put his hands on her shoulders, turned her over, and kissed her.

"Go on, go on," she said by mistake aloud, giving way with relief.

Gerald, however, made no attempt to remove her bikini. Making love in a hurry held no attractions for him and time and place were wrong. He was too conscious of Monica's imminent return.

"Juliet," he said, "do you take the Pill?"

"Of course, you nit."

"Then what are you doing here looking after my children? We'd better get things straight. Trouble with your boy friend?"

"In a way. But I don't want to talk about it." To discuss Oliver with another man would have been the ultimate treachery.

"Forget it then. Right?"

"You mean you'd like to make me," she said, angry at the interruption to her sensual processes. "What makes you think you can? And what about Monica? I like her."

"Monica understands. You needn't worry about what goes on between husband and wife, nothing can upset that. I don't ever pretend. Monica's the only person I'm permanently attached to. But it's quite possible to be devoted to one person and want passionately to make love to someone else. Most women don't understand, but you're much too intelligent not to. Lovemaking can be intensely exciting just for itself, but there must be respect. I could never be interested in casual sex, or insult a woman by offering it to her."

"You're wrapping things up in a lot of words," Juliet said. "Either you want to or you don't." By now she had got used to her shock, and her mind, fully awake, was saying why not? If Oliver had Lucy why shouldn't she have Gerald? It was foolish to be faithful to a hope. And why be one down? But she was furious for being made to give herself away, and then left with the pain of unsatisfied desire. She said coldly "If you make me stop and think about it I don't know that I care for the idea. I can see too many complications. Fine for you Monica doesn't mind, I hope it's true, I wouldn't touch you if I thought she did. But I don't fancy being made love to by courtesy of. And finish if you talked about me to Monica."

"I promise not."

"Well I'm promising nothing."

"No?" Delighted by her anger he kissed her again. Across his diaphragm, filling his solar plexus was the marvellous feeling he could have her when he wanted. Saturday? Everyone would be at the fête. "It's time we went back to the house. I heard the car. Don't be so alarmed, no one can see us. I look down this avenue every morning of my life from our bedroom, so I know."

48

But Harriet had been watching them for the last five minutes, seated on a hatbox in front of one of the attic windows.

Gerald took no account of this part of the house. In his childhood the attics had been exclusive to servants and now all the rooms stood empty, doors opening on to bare boards, except for one, and that only housed trunks and discarded nursery furniture. He had no idea that Harriet, discovering this territory for herself, had adopted it for her own room and turned it into a home for her dolls.

Behind the shut window the room smelt of hot dry dust. Belinda, an expensive jointed doll, lay naked in the cradle with her eyes shut. Monica's old felt Highlander stood stiff-legged in the high chair. Sometimes in the parts of brother and sister, sometimes husband and wife, the dolls, when necessary, acted out a gross parody of human life.

"You're very naughty," she said, "giving Belinda a headache because of the au pair. You're to stop it at once, d'you understand? Never mind, Belinda, he doesn't mean it really. She doesn't want him anyway. She's got a boy friend called Oliver. She told me."

Thinking of Juliet—in the fountain, running away across the lawn—she turned to look out of the window. From up here the yew walk seemed to her like two keys back to back. The rose gardens were their two round heads, the straight yew hedges the shafts, the square enclosures above the ha-ha were the wards and the peacocks the tips of the keys that go first into the lock. Harriet expected the wards to be empty, but there in the righthand key were her father and Juliet lying side by side. Riveted by curiosity and fear Harriet watched him roll on top of Juliet and begin to kiss her.

The Highlander fell forgotten to the floor. Harriet leant forward to see better.

49

She had often seen animals copulating, it was a common-place sight on the farm. She knew it was the same with people. Was this what her father was doing with Juliet now? She couldn't see what was going on underneath him. She waited for them to come apart.

But when they disentangled he was fully dressed, his trousers done up. His thing wasn't showing. When the bull got off the cow, his was swinging long and thin and red. Juliet still had on her bikini.

So they hadn't. Harriet let out her breath.

But her heart was bumping and she sat still, in terror, thinking of what might come next.

Suppose they did do it, somewhere where she couldn't see?

Would it mean divorce? She'd learned about this at school. Her friend Charlotte had divorced parents and had explained in some detail what happened, before and after. Charlotte lived with her mother, who had married again. Now there was two of everything it was horrible.

Harriet imagined what it would be like to live parted from her father, her throat constricted with misery. Rage followed, at the idea of Juliet having the Hall while the rest of them were sent away. She felt her mother's desolation now, in advance. Her heart swelled, she thought her chest would burst.

"Tea."

She heard Martin coming to find her. Not wanting him in here, she went downstairs.

"Tea," Monica called, coming out of the kitchen. "Tea, Gerald." She opened the library door.

She knew before going inside that the room was empty. On his desk the papers were neatly tidied as if they had been deliberately abandoned, and the cap had been put back on his pen. Looking out of the window and wondering where he was she saw him coming through the rose garden with Juliet. Their heads were bent inwards towards each other, like two magnets, a little more and they would click together. Through the fountain's veil Monica watched till they passed out of sight round the end of the terrace. She thought in pain how many times she had seen him sit through a dinner party next to some woman he was sleeping with and never give anything away. He must be thrown off his balance; this must mean more to him. When he was courting her he had been careless too. An immense sadness filled her. 'The fountain's weeping for me,' but they were cool, impersonal tears, endless and without pity.

Everyone was quiet at tea. Harriet was so pale that Monica, roused for the moment out of her preoccupation, wondered if the child had had too much sun.

"After tea I'll read to you if you like, in the drawingroom," she said. "I think you've both done enough running about."

"I want to play with Juliet," Martin said.

"It's Juliet's afternoon off. She's not really supposed to be here."

"I'm sorry. I didn't know. It seemed too hot to go out."

"That's all right. It's up to you. But if you're here it's difficult for the children to understand."

"Please read, but there's something I must just do first," Harriet said. "Not running about."

"All right. Come and find me in the kitchen when you're ready."

"What is it? Can I come?"

"No Martin, you can't. It's private."

Under an apple tree in the orchard Harriet placed a jam jar filled with cow parsley and herb robert. Her arms were yellow with pollen. She lifted them above her head and prayed for Juliet to go away.

7

Mrs Webster's train arrived at the station at ten minutes past four. One on either side of Gerald, the children danced up and down on the platform, waiting for her to appear. Three other people got out.

"There she is, there she is. Granny!" Harriet shouted.

A blue rinsed head topped by a nest of navy blue petals looked once up and down the platform and disappeared again. A gloved hand waved.

Mrs Webster emerged from the train bottom first, a thin neat bottom in navy blue, above thin elegant legs and black patent shoes. She paid no attention to her family. Her hands were stretched back towards the carriage to receive an endless series of suitcases, baskets, paper bags, coats and magazines. Not till the door shut and the train departed carrying off the pressganged helpers did she turn round and offer a cheek to be kissed.

"Darlings," she said.

The cheek was leathery. She wasn't sixty but all trace of sex had gone out of her face and she might have been any age. The dignity of grannydom suited her very well, according with the deference she considered her due. Her sharp blue eyes missed nothing.

"Martin, you have grown. What a big boy. And Harriet gets prettier every time I see her. She's going to be a beauty, Gerald." Her upper class voice rang through the station with the forceful clarity born of not caring who else hears because they don't count. "Now you shall take me to the car."

Gerald noticed with amusement and disgust that although

fashion now decreed that skirts should fall, Mrs Webster had only just reached the point of defiantly raising hers to display two little drumstick knobs. Knees had never been his mother's strong point.

She gave one hand to each child, and leaving her luggage on the platform far behind her for Gerald to cope with, made off through the side entrance, bypassing the ticket collector.

"Granny," Martin said from the back seat. "What have you brought?"

"You shouldn't ask. It's not polite," Harriet said hypocritically.

"You must wait and see. That's a secret," their grandmother answered.

"Mrs Barden's Betty's pregnant," Gerald announced. "I might as well tell you because you'll notice the moment you clap eyes on her. Mrs B's upset. We're marrying Betty off to George next month."

"Gerald! Not in front of the children!"

"Harriet had bad dreams last night. She had to go into Mummy's bed. All the doors banged," Martin said.

"Martin gets into Juliet's bed. I saw him in there asleep. They play pillowfights." Harriet's voice rose.

"Aren't you getting rather a big boy for that, Martin?" Mrs Webster turned round to look at him.

"Rubbish, Mother. She's a very nice girl. It's a very suitable bed for him to get into. Now, you two, if you start quarrelling in the back I'll stop the car and you can walk home."

Both children felt betrayed.

The big front door was open. Side by side in the doorway Juliet and Monica waited for the car to disgorge. Each preoccupied with her own thoughts and embarrassed by the other's company, together and in silence they had prepared tea and shucked peas. Juliet was trying to reconcile being in love with Oliver, wanting to sleep with Gerald, and liking Monica. Monica had given up all attempt to sort out her

54

feelings, and she wished Juliet at the bottom of the sea. She asked herself 'Why didn't I send her home the day she arrived?' Yet she was grateful to Juliet for being there beside her; in her present troubled state she couldn't face Gerald's mother without support. Mrs Webster and her weapons would leave Juliet unmoved, their orbits were too far apart.

Mrs Webster stepped out of the car and kissed Monica on both cheeks. "Darling, how cool you always manage to look."

"Tea's in the diningroom, Mother, when you're ready. This is Juliet, she's very kindly helping us with the children."

Without troubling to look at Juliet, Mrs Webster murmured, extending a hand, and continued her conversation with Monica. Then she swept slowly up the stairs, followed by Gerald with suitcases, and the children tottering under minor baggage.

'What a bitch,' Juliet thought. As they turned together to go back into the hall she caught Monica's eye, and involuntarily understanding passed between them.

The door of the spare room shut in the children's faces.

"No, not just yet. You must wait till I've changed."

Alone, Mrs Webster looked around her with distaste. For generations this room had been the day nursery, and it was still redolent, and always would be, of Gerald's infancy; of Nanny, the one person she had never been able to bend, of baby powder and hot nappies on the guard. Every time Monica put her to sleep here she felt herself offered a deliberate insult. The convenience of private entry to the visitors' bathroom, the fine view down the yew walk, did nothing to mitigate her displeasure. She approved neither the curtains, nor the flowers on the table, nor the colour of the carpet. No matter how Monica chose to doll the room up the fact remained that she had had no business in the first place to change its use. It was one of her many failings as a daughter-in-law.

Under cover of the noise of rustling tissue paper the children whispered on the landing.

"You shouldn't 've told about Juliet. You're horrid. I'll tell about you. I saw you in the orchard. I heard. Why d'you want her to go away? Rotten old cow parsley in a rotten old jam jar. Nothing's going to listen to that."

"If you tell, you don't love Mummy best. That means you're a traitor. If you're a traitor you have your head cut off. Then Rex and Janus will come and drink your blood."

"Juliet won't let you. Magic's wicked."

The door opened.

"Now, darlings, you can come in. I'm all ready."

Both children were smiling, anticipating presents. Mrs Webster put Martin's pallor down to excitement, and the unnatural stimulus of Juliet's bed.

"What have you brought for Juliet?" Martin said.

"Juliet's not family, darling. Now, aren't you going to take me down to tea?"

The presence of Mrs Webster made everyone behave formally, except for the children, who were given up to greed. Sensing the atmosphere and aligning herself with the inmates against the visitor, Juliet changed for dinner into a white dress brought with a view to such occasions and was ready to play Mrs Webster at her own game.

"You look like a bride," Gerald said when she appeared in the drawingroom. "Sherry or gin and tonic?"

"Sherry." She could think of nothing else to say. The way he was looking at her was too sexual, she was suddenly aware that he was handsome, and already Monica and Mrs Webster were crossing the hall, tinkling with conversation.

Tonight there were candles in the silver candlesticks on the diningroom table, not yet lit because out of doors the light was only just draining from the sky. Monica was in her proper place at the foot of the table; opposite Juliet Mrs Webster sat on Gerald's right. Her long thin hands, loaded with good rings, unfolded her table napkin and straightened the cutlery in front of her with deft touches. She hadn't missed the look in her son's eye as he handed Juliet her sherry. So that's what he wants now. She noted the fact.

Long ago she had forgotten what passion felt like, but in spite of her own coldness and rigid sense of propriety, she knew that the bull must have his heifers. Gerald, as a really pedigree bull, had, on principle, a right to the best, and as many as he chose. In his case she would have considered droit de seigneur perfectly in order.

This was a pretty girl, and reasonably presentable.

"Where do your parents live, dear?" she inquired.

"In Hove."

"How pleasant. They're retired, I suppose."

"Oh no, my father works there. He has a bookshop. I'm afraid we don't cultivate a family tree, we're very ordinary."

For a moment Mrs Webster looked taken aback.

"You must give me the address. Then I can get him to send me the latest Agatha Christie."

"You don't read your paper, Mother. Juliet's father deals in rare books. She's got her eye on our library for him. All the best books are going absent one by one. But I'm afraid it's no go, Juliet. There are one or two there I want myself."

Mrs Webster changed tack. "And where were you at school?"

"Juliet's up at Oxford."

"How interesting. Gerald was at Cambridge, weren't you darling? How fortunate for you to be able to go to the Varsity. Of course it's much easier for young people now, there were no grants in my day."

Gerald waited to see how his mother would get out of committing one or other of the cardinal sins—talking about money, or about rank.

"In any case, in our circle, girls didn't go to college. We were presented. Quite fun, but not so good for our minds."

In some subtle way Monica had ceased to count. Mrs Webster had taken command and was turning her side of the table into the head, mounting a sub fusc battle against her son. Gerald felt the pressure. His face was a map of anxiety, all the lines scored and running downwards.

"The children are very excited about the fête," she said. "I suppose it will be in the paddock, Gerald?"

"Certainly not. Where on earth d'you think we'd put the cars? In the drive? And have everyone tramping through the rose garden? And who'd clear up the mess afterwards? It'll be in the field by the village hall."

"Don't you think you're making a mistake, dear?"

"No Mother I don't. And don't tell me my father would never have allowed such a thing. He's been dead now for over thirty years, and you weren't married to him for long enough to know what he thought about anything." There was a stunned silence. "Besides that's where the village wants to have it. They like to feel free to make a noise, and there's a dance afterwards."

"Preferring the village hall! I don't know what the lower classes are coming to."

"I'm quite sure you don't."

"I didn't think upper and lower classes existed any more," Juliet said with deliberate innocence. "Does anyone really believe in them still? There's nothing now except richer and poorer."

"My dear Juliet, if you don't mind my saying so, that's a townswoman's view. It shows you've never had much to do with the country. If you don't believe me, go to the social in the hall tomorrow night and get among Mrs Barden and her friends. They'll be very polite, but you'll be put in your place firmly and expected to stay there. Monica is on very matey terms with everyone at the w.i., but they know and she knows where she stands, and that's how they want it. They make a distance they don't want you to cross. My family has been here for centuries but we're still invaders to the real inhabitants. We're accepted because we know what's expected of us and do it, but however much we sweat our guts out for it even we shall never be so much part of the place as they are. It's not a question of cash or cars, it's who's been here longest. And that's the lower class. Saxon serfs. Monica and Mother have an honourable status here as wives, but they'll never be natives like Harriet and Martin. And Mother's opted out by going to live in Eastbourne."

"What nonsense you do talk, Gerald."

"I still don't think you're right," Juliet said.

The light was beginning to go, the last rays lit up her hair, gold against the dark panelling. Her white dress shone luminous, her skin was an invitation to touch. Gerald and his mother were both looking at her in such a predatory way that Monica was almost afraid to leave the room to get the sweet in case when she came back she would find Juliet in shreds on the floor, torn to pieces by their eyes.

Mrs Webster had been visited by a major thought.

"Monica, dear," she said, putting a spoon to her raspberry ice, "while I'm here, don't you think it would be a good opportunity for you to have a little rest, and take a few days holiday on your own? I'm sure Juliet's very capable with the children and I can take care of the house."

"I don't think it a good idea at all. Really, Mother, I should see nothing of you."

Gerald got up from his chair to light the candles. Their pale flames fought with the dusk outside till at last they married with it, drawing those round the table closer together. In leaning past Juliet his hand brushed her shoulder. Monica saw this and wondered if her present hell would ever end.

"About the children, Gerald," Mrs Webster was saying. "Surely it's time Martin learnt to ride? It's not fair on him you know, not to have him taught. He ought to hunt and he ought to shoot, and you can't start to learn too young."

"Can't you! I'm not having my son tortured in the way I was. If, and when, he wants to learn to ride, he can have a pony. But I'll not have this nonsense of hunting at six and seeing beautiful creatures torn to pieces. Not for Martin. I can still remember being blooded. I felt sick for days and you thought it such a treat, didn't you? I suppose it wouldn't occur to you that some children are frightened of horses. Nor is any child of mine going to be let loose with a gun before he's ten. A shotgun's a lethal weapon. I know every farmer's got to be able to shoot, but not little boys of his age." He pushed back his chair. "What about coffee, Monica?"

"Don't let's argue," Monica said. "Let's play bridge, now we've got a four. I'll bring the coffee into the drawingroom. I expect you play, don't you Juliet?"

"I'm afraid I don't. I'm so sorry."

But to Mrs Webster bridge was a drug. "We can play cut throat," she said. "Fun."

The three faces concentrated round the green baize table top were wiped clear of all emotion. Their eyes were on the cards. Nothing was said irrelevant to the game. Stretches of silence were interrupted by monotone bidding; there was little dissection of play. Feeling like a ghost Juliet left the room, opening and shutting the door softly, not even saying goodnight.

As soon as she turned on her bedroom light a moth flew in at the window. It was large and white, with a furry body, thin delicate legs and enormous eyes shining red. She switched the light off again to prevent it from banging itself to pieces and leant over the windowsill into the hot black night. The moth was invisible now and its fluttering drowned by the ceaseless fountain.

No letter from Oliver had come. The moth was a messenger. All the way from Turkey, from beside Lucy, Oliver's deep liquid brown eyes, that conveyed such an unfair impression of vulnerability were reproaching her. If Oliver was hurt it was his own fault for hurting her. For a moment Juliet was seized by panic and she saw just how much she would mind if her

60

gamble didn't come off and Oliver never found Lucy out. Then she gave desire full rein, interposing Gerald and sensation as a shield between herself and her deepest feelings.

The heavy voluptuous night carried argument away, making decision unnecessary. Her body lost its boundaries and flowed out to become one with the dark. It was a long time before she moved.

Down below, away to the left, the light from the drawing-room window lay in a yellow bar across the grass. Moved by pity for the pain she had seen in Gerald's face during dinner she was glad he was having a respite. She draw her curtains, undressed and got into bed.

'With that mother here nothing can happen anyway,' she thought.

The moth had gone.

It was one thirty when the bridge players came upstairs. Juliet had been asleep for three hours.

8

At the top of the stairs Juliet turned and looked back. Monica was standing by the landing window arranging roses in a bowl on the half-moon table.

"Oh yes you'd better go. We shan't have any peace if you don't," she had said.

She was wearing a blue and white cotton frock that showed off her skin, which never burnt and never browned but stayed a pale olive white. Her whole aspect, her fingers playing with the flowers, was patrician, belonging to any century.

The landing window was designed to provide a view for those coming upstairs, and the passage leading to it was a broad enclave bounded by the blank walls of Monica's bedroom to the right and the best spare room to the left, where Mrs Webster was holding court from her bed. Across the landing between Juliet and Monica the main upstair passage ran the length of the house. The roses in the bowl were deep red, illuminating the vista from the stairs.

'How can anybody be so calm? How can anybody be so passive? If it was my mother-in-law I'd tell her where she got off. I'd make her wait for her paper,' Juliet thought, hurrying downstairs in an effort to create movement in the static atmosphere.

Monica stayed looking out of the landing window, pretending to arrange the roses in the cut glass bowl. Juliet was now on her way to the village. The children were hovering round their grandmother's bed.

Immediately below, the top of the fountain's watery umbrella was constantly in play and beyond, the yew walk led the eye away into the distance. Today the fountain she always thought of as particularly part of her said nothing to her at all. Usually its gentle voice was an affirmation; telling her over and over again that past and future were alike and that her way of life was at one with them, a process of continual renewal. Her naiads, perpetually submitting to the water's flow, were closer to her than sisters. But now they were remote, their message withheld.

The whole of her system had received such a shock that her personality was shattered. She felt as if she was a looking glass smashed to a thousand pieces, and because she could no longer see what she was like, she couldn't begin to put herself together again.

'Gerald ought to mend me,' she thought. 'But it was him who did this.'

There was no glass under this roof for her to look in, no still water to reflect back her image. Gerald's agonised face showed nothing but his own trouble and evasion, while in Mrs Webster's eyes all she could read was a calculating wish for her disintegration to be complete. Juliet and the children didn't see her at all.

Faintly from behind the blind wall their high voices rose and fell.

'The only person who can help me now is Simon.'

Simon was completely outside, an exotic bird watching from a jungle tree. Hour after hour she had sat in front of him undisguised. Of course, Simon would know how the pieces went. In his parlour there was no need for mental clothes.

She got into the car and tore up the drive, shutting her mind against what she knew quite well, that it should have been Gerald she opened her mouth to and that this expedition was a mistake born of despair.

Usually she left the car in the road outside Simon's little black and white house and walked up the path to the front door. Today, not wanting to encounter Juliet, she drove up the track that led to his garage and tucked the car out of sight by the back door. The pigeons from the loft over the garage rose in clouds, to settle again as soon as she switched off the engine. Her misgivings rose and fell with them. The noise of hoovering came from indoors. Simon had once said "I'm a wailing wall for your sex, ducky," and she was afraid of finding herself in that company. So far she had done all the listening.

The hoovering stopped with a whine. 'I feel as if I was going to the dentist. This is ridiculous. It's only Simon.' The back door opened.

He was a tall man, with narrow hips, broad shoulders and grey curly hair. His face was triangular, if anything putty-coloured, and he always gave Monica the impression of being flat, like a picture. He was wearing a faded purple shirt, espadrilles, and pale blue jeans too tight across the buttocks for his age.

"Monica! Darling! Just the person. No of course you're not interrupting. Come in and we'll have a nice cup of tea. What a fate! I've got three thousand words to rehash for my mag, getting rid of a little illegit, and it's no use suggesting abortion because they won't wear that in the mags. I was in town yesterday and I said to my editor 'Not one little teeny illegit, ducky?' and she said 'Not in such a light jolly vein, please, Simon. The girl must *suffer*.'

"And Harry's gone darling, so no one to cook, and one's heart in shreds."

"But you mustn't upset your fans. Poor Simon. I'm in trouble too."

"Vi, I suppose. I saw the old lizard in the village. I don't know how Gerald stands his mother. That woman should have been strangled the minute she had given birth."

"No. Not that she's not bad enough. It's something else."

Simon's eyes strayed. He put on the kettle and fussed with cups.

"No, please, Simon you must listen, to me, for once, or I'll go mad."

He was as elusive as the child in the watercolour over the mantelpiece, whose tight yellow curls and lace ruffles were neither male nor female.

"Don't do that ducky. That would be a mistake. Well, tell then. But if you're worried about Gerald and Rachel I won't believe you. What a female. Leaning over her gate smirking, large as life and twice as nasty."

"Oh Rachel! *No*, Simon!" But when she put her worry about Juliet into words it sounded lame.

"I don't know what you're fussing about," and now Simon's reptilian face was withdrawn from her like all the others. "Gerald's used to having any woman he fancies, he's got conditioned reflexes, like a laboratory dog, he can't help himself. The only difference this time is that it's happening under your roof so you see all the moves."

"But if it's the same why doesn't he talk to me about it?"

"It's a very unsanitary habit. But seriously, ducky, you're not using your head. You told Gerald no Juliet. He just *has* to have her. He knows quite well if he tells you you'll say no and then he'll be in a jam. So he says nothing. Right? And don't forget it's a new thing for him too, having his girl in the house. Very throwing. But if you can't stand it send the girl away. It's no good having all these ladylike scruples."

"But Gerald would never forgive me for not trusting him."

"That, ducky, is rubbish. He'd be flattered. Has he slept with her yet?"

"I don't think so."

"Then what are you waiting for? Give her the push quick. The whole thing is rubbish, but if you're jealous, send her packing. Never play games with jealousy, ducky. Now I'm going to give you your pelargonium cutting I've been saving up for you and turn you out. Plant it in a sunny place and give it some water, then you can bring it in at the end of the summer and have all those lovely bi-coloured flowers to remember me by."

"Oh Simon!"

"There's Vi with your brats, dripping ice cream. Shall we shout?"

Monica drew back and hid behind him. "No. Please. I couldn't bear her just now."

When Mrs Webster was out of sight Monica drove off in the opposite direction, inventing errands to ensure that she arrived home alone.

"After all the hours I've spent holding his hand. Even drying his tears. He doesn't want to listen! I don't rush out in the middle of his telling me about his hairy sailors."

The first time she had met Simon he had been standing in the middle of his art nouveau blue and green sittingroom with tears cutting ditches in the make-up covering his face. She was surprised because it all seemed quite natural.

"Have my hanky. Or shall I go away?" she said. "Look, you'd better let me. You're making a terrible mess. D'you want me to put on a new face?"

"No dear. Thanks. I've done with it. Oh well, that's the end of that." He took the hanky from her and blew his nose. "How sweet you are. This is all very shaming. Please don't be put off." With astonishment he took in her twin set and pearls, and acute interest in the disparity between her appearance and behaviour got the better of his distress. "Why aren't you put off? Who are you? Please come again. Don't just vanish, now will you?"

"Why should I be put off?" Monica said.

With mounting excitement she saw the possibility of making a friend. What's more he was a sort of person barred to her so far, who could open the door into fields of experience where the rules she'd been brought up to follow didn't run. Meeting him made her feel how narrow her life was.

She said to Gerald that evening "That new person at Little

67

Orchard is rather nice. We ought to have him to dinner."

"If you must. But I can't stand queers."

So she called again casually, and kept the friendship to herself.

By now Simon was necessary to her. Gerald, directly in bed and through his descriptions of other women, introduced her to a wide variety of normal sexual behaviour. Her intimacy with Simon took her inside the deviant's mind. At first he was fairly reticent, but when Monica asked questions he unbuttoned. He went into his rape and spurn relationships with lorry drivers and sailors, deliberately leading her on till at last he became careless, taking aggressive pleasure in telling her the most intimate physical details. So behind her polite face she collected from the two men vicarious sex of both kinds and experience of a great deal of life she couldn't lead.

But today Simon had withdrawn all he'd previously given her. At the same time he'd taken a bit of herself to keep. Like a witch stealing a piece of hair so as to have power over her. Then he'd closed the door in her face.

This was too frightening to accept. 'I'm seeing it upside down. It was the wrong time for me to call; he's got all those words to think up and type out before the post goes. He didn't mean to be unkind, he was trying to help. What he said was quite commonsense. If necessary of course I can send Juliet away.'

But she felt worse and not better; by mentioning her problem somehow she had lowered her marriage and put Juliet at a remove. To her surprise she thought 'I like her. Really I would have liked to know her better. I don't want her to go away.' And this was frightening too.

9

Juliet came back from the village unhappy and walked down the drive, in and out of the shade under the chestnut trees. It was light dark light dark hot cold alternately, but she was too angry to notice.

From his seat on the tractor Gerald had seen her go up the drive. Since breakfast he had been baling hay in the field beyond the pond. It was a job he loved and he was deeply happy. Waiting for her to come back again he was thinking lovingly of laying her. When he saw her turn into the drive he stopped the tractor and strolled over to the gate.

"I've just been having a drink with your trollop," was what she said and walked on, his mother's newspaper crumpled to a baton in her hand.

Gerald watched Juliet's unrelenting back while his fury boiled. Fury that any young woman working in his house should dare to speak to him in such terms, fury with Rachel for breaking every known code: that was a cunt he should have left alone. Fear that he had lost his gorgeous piece of nougat supervened. 'Kicked in the balls,' he thought, going back to his tractor. Work didn't answer. Prompted by the sight of the church tower every time he turned a row, he stopped the tractor and walked across the intervening fields.

There was absolute stasis inside the church. Day in day out the effigy of Thomas Ingram, incorporated by Gerald as a small boy among his ancestors, slept on his tomb with his ankles crossed. Winter and summer the banners hung motionless over the altar. Solace was always forthcoming. In this one place all his desires and functions were understood: Gerald the landowner, Gerald the lover, husband, son, everything. He could show his naked soul without fear of rebuff. But the deep peace that descended on him vanished as he came out again into the hot sun. He was left chaotic and miserably lonely. This wound he could not take to Monica.

Rachel had kidnapped Juliet outside the post office as easily as picking a baby out of its pram.

"What about drinkies? You look parched," she had said.

A toy leopard dangled in the back window of the car; Juliet recognised the two tone horn as the same that had summoned Gerald from the greenhouse and eaten up by curiosity got in without another thought.

Everything in Rachel's garden looked plastic: the uniform red roses, even the blue water in the swimming pool. It didn't need a gnome because it had Rachel. The curve of her arm pouring gin was voluptuous yet not quite blowsy, but too white, her glossy back hair reminded Juliet of enamel. She pinned Juliet down in a chaise longue with a glass of gin and proceeded venomously to tell her all about Gerald, destroying him as neatly as a wasp nips the wings off a fly.

"And don't pretend you're smarter than the rest of us. You'll open your legs if he asks you to," she finished. "Don't say I didn't warn you."

It had been difficult for Juliet to dispose of her glass, get up and walk away with any sort of dignity.

'Let him fry, he's a con,' she thought as she left Gerald behind and the Hall came in sight smugly perfect among its trees. 'All that high flown chat. Not interested in casual sex! What else could that woman be? I'm not willing to be anybody's tart.'

The hurt administered by both men exploded inside her. 'I'll go and pack. Fuck the lot of them. What's to keep me? I'll find someone else somewhere else.'

"So you're here at last. Put the paper in my room, will you? On the writingtable." Mrs Webster passed out of the front door, the children trailing behind her.

'I'm not your housemaid, either,' Juliet thought and her resolution hardened.

Opening the spare room door she wondered how Mrs Webster had managed to produce anything as sensual as Gerald. Under her occupation the room had taken on overtones of Eastbourne and its very smell changed. The nightdress case, a violet in mauve silk embroidered in one corner, was instantly reminiscent of hotel bedspreads; her monogrammed silver-backed hair brushes sat on the dressingtable with a temporary air. Bedroom slippers were neatly placed for the convenience of a chambermaid. She had succeeded in subduing all trace of the romance inherent in the house. With repugnance Juliet put the newspaper down on the writing table. The crumples were past praying for. 'I'll be gone before she has a chance to complain.'

A faintly nagging conscience towards Monica impelled her to go down to the kitchen, but Mrs Barden with barely concealed hostility said "Madam has gone out and won't be back till lunch." On the kitchen transistor someone was singing "I wanna hole your ha-a-n."

'That's it then,' Juliet thought and slammed her suitcase on to her bed. The damaged copy of *Beowulf* made her feel trapped, cut off from her contemporaries in all this false gentility and she put it quickly in the bottom righthand corner. 'Let me out let me out. Back to my own kind. I'll sew on his buttons, make him baked beans on toast, black Lucy's eye.'

But back to where? Hove? Wait in a teashop or work in a factory?

The contents of the chest of drawers were soon packed. With her white frock folded on the bed Juliet paused.

'This is the only address he has. Suppose he writes? I shall never get his letter. Suppose he comes and finds me gone?' Each week stretching ahead till the Michaelmas term began in October seemed as long as a whole year. 'Why do I have to love him? The only thing is to wait here. I've no choice. Oh well then, sweat it out.'

The white frock went back on its hanger. Packing and going away was an unnecessary gesture, three sizes too big for Gerald. He was not worth so much resentment. It came to her that in any case she was the person in control of this situation, because she didn't care two pins for him, nor did she believe that sex had to be wrapped up and labelled to be acceptable. Poor man! As the gloss Gerald and the Hall had surreptitiously collected fell away, all traces of guilt towards Oliver and Monica vanished. Juliet noticed it was a marvellous day; made for sunbathing, but no time before lunch. She wondered why Gerald had to have Rachel when he had a wife as attractive as Monica? Perhaps after a surfeit of Country Life you felt you had to go and make love to a garden gnome among garden gnomes. Very likely Monica was inhibited, love wasn't polite.

After all Monica was stuffed with ideas of class and what was Done and Not Done, and that generation was hopeless about sex anyway. She'd probably never heard of the Kama Sutra, let alone tried any of it.

The bedroom door was moving. "Whichever child that is, go away. I know it's lunch and I'm coming," she said, abandoning her unpacking till later.

Monica found all these faces round the lunch table very strange. Martin was chalk white, Harriet like a cat who has been at the cream, Juliet detached, Gerald wretched and Mrs Webster suffused with predatory excitement.

"We've been kite flying but it was no good," announced Harriet.

"The kite wouldn't fly," Martin said. "It didn't get up off the ground."

His grandmother reprimanded him at once. "It's rude to complain about presents, the kite will fly when there's a wind. Don't play with your food. Sit straight and eat up your dinner."

"He's had too much ice cream," Harriet said. "It always makes him feel sick."

Monica could tell at once from Harriet's tone of voice that she was lying. It was something else that had upset Martin. What?

Juliet cleared the plates away and Gerald made towards the door, but Mrs Webster stopped him.

"I want a word with you," she said. "Upstairs in my room."

"I suppose if you must. All right. When I've had coffee." He was mourning the marvellous golden auburn bush he was now perhaps never going to see, convinced more than ever that it would be red rather than blonde.

'What's been going on?' Monica thought. 'This house isn't mine any more. These people are all dolls. There's no place for me anywhere. I don't know about definitions of hell but as far as I'm concerned this is it.' She was not comforted by Gerald's suffering. 'He's only got to get down on his knees on a hassock and he's ready for the next round.'

10

Gerald walked upstairs still thinking about Juliet's bush. He knew it must be large, because when she was sunbathing he had seen a few curling hairs straying out from under her bikini. The prospect of having to listen to what was on his mother's mind filled him with acute boredom. It was a scene that had been played regularly since his childhood, always from her bed, ostensibly for his good or that of the family, and singularly inapposite now.

She was already under the eiderdown, propped up against the pillows, her leathery neck and face rising above the frills of a bright pink négligé. She seemed all the more desiccated by contrast with the vivid picture of Juliet that filled his mind. As usual, his mother was trying to look frail. But really she was as strong as any man, with himself apparently upright at the foot of her bed but in essence supine, in the inferior position.

They were two antagonists measuring up against each other, two fencers studying each other warily through their masks, but, in spite of the masks, with the buttons off their foils. The expressions on their faces were singularly alike.

"Well, Mother," Gerald said. "What is it this time?"

"Don't fidget, dear, there's something I want to say to you."

"Get on with it then."

"Don't you think Monica is seeing rather a lot of Simon?"

Gerald turned cold inside. For a moment he was terrified. 'She wants to take Monica away from me and this will destroy me. She wants to kill me. She must hate me.' Then he laughed at the implicit absurdity.

"I don't think you should take it so lightly. He may be only

75

a writer, but he's a very attractive man. I saw her this morning coming out of his house. I wouldn't have thought anything of it, but she was trying to prevent my seeing her. And this is not the first occasion. People are going to Talk. I think you should Say Something To Her. It would be different if you went there together, but you never speak to him. Now do you?"

"That pouf! I should hope not. Kindly leave Monica alone. It wouldn't worry me if I saw her coming out of his house with the milk. I will not tolerate your trying to interfere between me and my wife. There'll be serious trouble if you do."

"Very well. But I consider it was my duty, and I don't think it's very nice for the children. That was another thing Gerald. I really think it's time Harriet and Martin stopped sharing a bedroom. Martin is quite old enough now to go away to school. I had a very nice letter from Mr Peters last week, he has kept a place for him in September. So kind."

There was no pink left under the brown of Gerald's skin.

"Over my dead body. Martin is not going to boarding-school. No son of mine is going to suffer what I did. Or my daughter. The children are doing very well where they are."

"But Gerald, dear, if you don't send Martin to prep school he'll never get into Eton, and I don't know where you would find a better place than Chad House. Mr Peters is a dear. It's good for boys to have to stand on their own feet." She began to play chess with the objects on her bed, moving her book, the paper, her knitting, her writing case, permuting their positions. "Men should be men."

Gerald's spirits rose. 'I've got her on the hop. She's rattled.' He paused to swipe his mother on the minor point before moving to his major attack. "Martin's properly endowed and if he wasn't there's nothing Peters could do about it. We've got a perfectly good grammar school here."

"But Gerald! You *couldn't* do *that*! Send your children to the *grammar school*? *All* the Websters have *always* gone to Eton!"

Up to this moment it had never entered his head to do so; the perfect goad had been put into his head, usable for at least another ten years. His decision had been instantaneous.

"Educationally, grammar schools are very good. Ours is particularly satisfactory. There's a very fine record of university scholarships. Comfort yourself with the thought that public schools are not what they were, Mother. Far less flogging and bullying that in your day, or mine, so I'm led to believe."

"Think of the *people* they would meet!"

"Breeding always tells. My children aren't going to be contaminated by anyone. They'll meet a good cross section there, and these days you've got to learn to mix with all classes. Far more use to Martin than wasting time at Eton. I'm not proposing to send either of them to boarding school, but if I did, it would be to Dartington, not Eton. Or Benenden for that matter."

"But Dartington's one of those modern co-educational places!" Two carmine dots appeared, one on each cheekbone.

"That's the point."

"I don't understand you Gerald."

"You never have done."

"But what will people think? What can I say to them?"

"I can't imagine. You'll have to make something up. You're very good at that." This took him back, with almost the same pleasure, to the day when he had been discovered making love to the Rector's niece in her own bed during a game of hide and seek, and his mother had been forced, against all her principles, to fight on his side. "Now Mother, I'm afraid I must go. I've got a busy day."

His upbringing had been too thorough for him to be able to slam the door.

'She never could take sex,' he thought, going downstairs two steps at a time, 'she thinks she worships the male, but she'd be happier if there were no balls left in the world. Then where would she be for her precious heirs?"

Mrs Webster's hands lay quite still. How handsome her son was! But what a pity he hadn't Simon's manners! What a pity he was married to Monica!—a useless creature; neither one thing nor the other; neither aristocratic enough to keep him up to the mark, nor plebeian enough to be kept in her place. It was a great mistake she had not been put there from the start.

Almost any decorative little girl would have been more suitable. The perfect solution sprang fully armed into her head. Why not Juliet? Why not? Monica would be divorced and would marry Simon, of course. Gerald would marry Juliet and beget more babies. That would keep him occupied. She herself would return to the Dower House and take charge of the children of the first marriage. Then Martin would go to boarding school and there would be an end to this softness. No more nonsense. She would bring him up in the way he should go. She visualised the grown man: handsome, grateful, loving, correct, marrying the right girl. On Martin rested the future of the line. She began to go over the Dower House in her mind, re-allocating the rooms. It only remained to prize Gerald and Monica apart.

Subconsciously the centre of her parasitical love was shifting from her son to her grandson.

She sighed. Gerald was becoming more intractable with the years, not less.

"Wrong, wrong, wrong," Martin followed Harriet up and down the terrace, chanting to the tune of *Three Blind Mice*. "Wrong, wrong, wrong." He was drunk on the discovery that his sister was not infallible.

Vistas of liberation opened in front of him and he could even imagine that one day he might be big enough to hit her successfully. Juliet had not gone away.

His chant was not a taunt against Harriet so much as a hymn of praise to the world at large.

"She hasn't gone, she wasn't packing," he sang.

Harriet rounded on him. "She was. I saw her. There was a suitcase on her bed and she put *all* the things out of the chest of drawers in it."

"She didn't. When I looked there wasn't any packing."

"She did. I saw."

"She didn't."

"Did."

"Didn't."

"Did. Oh go away you nasty sneaky *little* boy."

Martin hit her with all his strength and with one push was felled to the terrace.

Mrs Webster stuck her head out of her bedroom window. "If you don't stop quarrelling at once and play quietly for half an hour there will be no picnic." And she withdrew it again.

Martin got up and went on singing to himself under his breath. Ignoring him, Harriet stood by the fountain scuffing bits of moss into the water with her sandal. She was philosophical about Juliet not going away, it was her own fault for telling Martin about the packing. If you told you broke the magic. She should have waited till Juliet was out of the house. Perhaps if the rain from the fountain wetted her skin without her sandal touching the water that would knit the magic up again. In an extended kick she held out her foot as far as she could. Two drops fell on her bare toes where they showed between the slats of her sandal. It was very difficult to keep her balance and that was why it could work. She didn't fall in. Her foot came back without touching the water in the basin.

So that was all right.

"If you want to play catch, Martin, why not fetch your ball?" she said kindly.

Gerald flung up the bottom sash of the library window. "Where's Juliet?"

"We don't know, do we Martin? Perhaps she's gone away."

"Don't talk such rubbish."

"She's in the kitchen. Helping Mummy make cakes," Martin said slowly. "When Granny's finished her rest we're going for a picnic. We're going to light a fire and bake potatoes."

"Well I hope you don't send the whole place up in flames."

"Don't be silly," Harriet said. "If you think we will why not come too? You never do anything with us. It's always you're too *busy*."

"So I am. At this time of year." The library window shuffled down.

Gerald was obsessed. During the last three days Juliet had assumed the desirability and inaccessibility of the Christmas tree fairy, who was never to be had. Leaning against the jamb of the kitchen door he decided she didn't look angry. But she didn't take any notice of him either, and her features were as clearly detached from her thoughts as if she were lunching with strangers in a restaurant.

Pinky-pong, pinky-pong. Are your balls hanging com-fut-a-bully? '*Listen With Mother* transposed,' he thought. A man ought to be allowed two wives, Monica wouldn't mind so long as she was head wife. Juliet, with her hands up to the wrists in a bowl of flour, mixing dough in his own kitchen, was giving him an erection. His prick sprang to life. He could feel the knob of it, starting small like a button mushroom, swell to monstrous size and the whole magnificent structure with it, growing at fantastic speed, like Alice. Its head hit the ceiling. In this case his trousers.

His discomfort was acute. There was the usual awkward transition from vertical downwards to vertical upwards, with a change of scale into the bargain.

80

Monica watched his trousers stretching like a sail. His manoeuvres to deal with this predicament had often amused her in the past. Today she saw nothing funny in them.

Ostensibly looking out of the window, he bent forward with his hands in his pockets while he effected the transfer. "The hedge needs cutting, Monica, I'll have to do something about it."

"Oh Gerald. You know it doesn't. There are masses more urgent things," she said, indicating she knew what he was at.

Uncomprehending, Juliet never looked up, missing the pantomime put on for her benefit. She could feel his attention bracketed on her and was determined to take no notice.

"Are either of you women going on this picnic?"

"No of course not. We've got the cakes to make for the fête."

"I don't trust Mother. The whole place is like tinder."

"Then you'd better go yourself."

"What about Juliet?" He was gazing at her like a dog asking to be taken out for a walk.

"Juliet's helping me for once," Monica said, thinking of the tomatoes. She was shocked to find there were two Monicas inside her. One was the controlled Monica she was used to, well-bred, well brought up; the other, a creature who reacted like a bitch on heat, and whose vulva, denied, hurt with frustration. In a strange unison these two were thinking 'His erection's for her, not me. This calm we've been having is quite false.'

Juliet's radiant detachment made the situation worse. 'It's gone to his head. If only Juliet had been come hither like all the others he'd soon have lost interest, he'd have seen to it there was no baby. But he means to have her. He wants to impregnate her and see more little Geralds come out of her womb, I know that look on his face. He's never looked at anyone but me like that before.' Anguish overcame her, a sense of being utterly abandoned. 'Your seed is mine. Not for her. It's mine. All mine.'

She caught Gerald's eye. It was happy and defiant; jaunty.

'He doesn't see me, I'm not real, I'm just Mummy.'

She felt herself having a brainstorm and was astonished that the other two didn't notice and exclaim. When it was over she was left with the seed of hitherto totally unsuspected violence growing inside her. She had stopped feeling civilised and it didn't surprise her. Though her polished shell remained the same, underneath it one Monica had swallowed the other.

"Oh well we'll have to let Mother and her picnic rip," Gerald said. "I'll leave you to it."

Juliet deliberately kept her eyes on her mixing bowl, spinning out what she was doing till she was sure he had gone. Whatever he might think, her legs and Rachel's were not the same thing. And some legs were foregiveable, others not. Rachel's definitely not. She took her hands out of the flour, about to ask for the milk.

Monica's face, white with strain, was as empty as the doorway she was staring at.

'She's had too much,' Juliet thought, 'it's that mother-in-law. And why do people have fêtes?'

"Do let me finish off here, you look exhausted. And about the fête, I really don't care if I go or not. Why not let me have the afternoon off tomorrow instead of Sunday? I'd like to look at the town and the shops'll be open then. Mrs Webster is sure to want to take the children round everything. I'd only be wasted. If I have tomorrow afternoon off I could give you the day in bed on Sunday."

'She's unconscious. Like a child bride,' Monica thought; 'she's insulated against me inside that radiance, I can't touch her. I can't even send her home. It's between Gerald and me. I must fight it out with him.'

"That's an idea," she said. "I don't care for staying in bed, but I would like to have the afternoon free with Gerald for once."

82

Monica's body responded as usual to Gerald's lovemaking but for the first time in her life she was watching herself perform. While physically on fire beyond control, emotionally she was frigid, her mind still ticking over, active and aloof. Was he taking so much trouble because he'd had Juliet already and was feeling guilty? Or was he practising? Even her own orgasm made her angry. If she'd not had one he might have noticed she was unhappy. 'But he knows me by heart, my body belongs to him, it's not me any more.' She lay awake. His arm, weighing heavy, pinned her down. Her unhappiness terrified her, she questioned everything. Nothing was certain any more. All the outlines in her life were fluid.

Gerald went to sleep at once, like a contented baby. His efforts had been totally genuine. All lovemaking was important to him. To his mind there should be no woman he couldn't satisfy. Every time he made love he proved his sexual supremacy. But the proof mattered most of all when he was with his wife. Planing above his vanity and the sequence of women in his life was his love for Monica, so fundamental it had never occurred to him it could be questioned.

11

"Don't think you'll ever make me forget Oliver."

"I'm not trying to. But I've made sure you'll never forget me."

Juliet and Gerald were lying naked on a rug at the edge of a cornfield. They were as snug as two partridges in stubble. The corn in front of them had not yet reached that stage, it was undulating silkily. There were still six weeks to go till harvest.

"Poppies! Aren't they beautiful."

"Not to me. Just bad farming."

"Where are we? I've lost track," she said dreamily.

"In one of my fields. Soon the corn will be the same colour as your hair."

"But you must have miles and miles of land! How ever far are we from the village? We were driving for ages."

"Not a bit of it. I was going round and round, waiting for your temper to subside. Besides, driving past waving corn has an aphrodisiacal effect. It's a well known country practice."

"You're a con," she said lazily, too happy to care.

"I'm sorry about Rachel. She was a mistake."

"You're sorry I found out. She was a ripe error."

He smiled. "Well I'm sorry you were let in for her."

"How d'you make out she was a Beautiful Sexual Experience? She's like one of those dummies in shop windows. Only worse, because she's soft."

"Skip Rachel," and Juliet knew that her curiosity would never be satisfied.

"Sex isn't the same thing as love," she said, bolstering herself against her own pleasure.

"Good Lord, I should hope not."

"Why 'hope not'?"

"It would make life far too complicated if you had to love everyone you made love with. The essence of a satisfactory love affair is non-commitment."

"That's rather chilly."

"Chilly? Not necessarily. It doesn't preclude fondness."

"How do you define love?"

"Commitment."

"So you're committed to Monica?"

"Naturally. And if you imagine you love that young man Oliver you should be committed to him, not to me."

"How right you are."

Now it was Gerald's turn to feel the draught. In the hot triumph of conquest he wanted the whole Juliet.

"Mark my words young woman, I'm telling you. Sex is an art, and in its own way just as important as love. I can give you something that young man has no conception of."

"Now I'm listening to the expert. Don't look sad. You'd hate it if I loved you. You can't have your cake and eat it."

"But I need to," he said quite seriously.

"What can I sell you?" Monica said, staring at Rachel's cleavage across the cake stall. Rachel's bosom was slung in a tight cup of pink and orange cotton, cut low. She was a natural part of the limbo of this fête; a place permeated by canned music that stunned thought, and filled with Gerald's ex-mistresses. Monica felt relegated and discarded as they were, pressed back among them by Gerald's most recent activity.

"I think one's always safe with a sponge," Rachel said, "I'll have that one."

'You're about number twenty,' Monica thought. She began to go round the stalls in her head, counting up the others on her fingers. At the jumble was No. 1 the Rector's niece, who had started the ball rolling, No. 2, the doctor's wife, was at the tombola, No. 3, the other doctor's wife, was judging the screaming babies, No. 4 led the pony. Her husband was the vet. At the far side of the field Mrs Webster had already managed to get Martin into the saddle. The animal's back was too broad for his short legs which stuck out stiffly on each side. He was clutching its mane and looking insecure. 'Poor mite. He's like me, wanting to be let off.'

Rachel's husband said "There's not much in a sponge, what about that fruit cake? That's more my style."

He was grosser than Rachel. His neck bulged sweatily above a silk cravat, his stomach overhung the tight band of his trousers.

"Bad for your waistline," Rachel said. "And probably heavy. You never know what's inside these cakes, they're made by anybody."

Monica had made the cake in question herself and knew that Rachel couldn't buy, and certainly could never make, a cake of such quality. Their discussion degraded her cake as she was degraded herself.

"Why not have both?" She felt herself part of a perverse game of Happy Families. Or of a harem at play; only most of the members didn't know who the others were. She had a hysterical desire to run round pinning little badges on them all, numbered 1, 2, 3, 4 and so on, like the circular identification discs people wear at conferences.

"Just the sponge," Rachel said. "By the way, where's Gerald? He passed us in the station wagon with that gorgeous au pair of yours, so we thought we'd be bound to find him here. John wants to have a word with him about getting a speed limit past our place. But he seems to have gone to ground."

Behind Rachel's shoulder Mrs Barden was listening to every word.

"I'm afraid you won't find him," Monica said coldly. "He had to go to the other side of the county on business and was dropping Juliet at the cinema on his way. In any case he never goes to fêtes. Yes, Mrs Barden, what can I do for you?" She turned her head so as not to witness Rachel's triumphant smile.

"I'll have half a dozen of them buns of yours please, madam, before they all go. I know them buns, and Miss Henderson said would I tell you she's on her way, but the tea tent's packed out and she got held up."

'In one minute flat I shall scream,' Monica thought. So Gerald had had it all wrapped up. He had never meant Juliet to get on that bus. It had been useless decanting her at the stop. She had looked so harmless standing there in the sun with a cardigan over one arm.

"Oh Monica! What luck! Give me that heavenly coffee icing one before someone else snaps it up." No. 6, the solicitor's wife.

The cakes were like so many consolation prizes dished out by herself to Gerald's other cast-offs. The happy morning packing them up in the kitchen seemed so long ago in time and space as to be an other-worldly heaven. There had been a festive air. Gerald sat on the table to drink his tea. Monica had felt happily normal.

"Mother's got Mrs Barden on the mat over Betty's pregnancy. As if she didn't know no one gets married here till they're pregnant."

"Don't worry. Mrs B. can hold her own. Their in-fighting has been going on ever since I can remember."

"So long as she doesn't give notice."

"Not on your life. Not with Betty getting married from here. By the time we've got rid of the confetti she'll have 'passed over' anything Mother says."

The perfect weather was still holding. Monica, looking forward to an afternoon devoted to Gerald and the family, with Juliet removed by a bus and not returning till bedtime, felt light as air. Functioning as lady of the manor didn't worry her, it served to relegate Juliet firmly to the au pair slot.

She said "Oh Gerald, before you go. I'm just taking these cakes down to the village, then we're having early lunch. Had we better take the station wagon as well this afternoon? Juliet's going out, so we shan't need it for room but I thought Mother might want to leave before I can get away."

"I'm not coming."

"Oh Gerald! But you must!"

Gerald's side of the conversation thudded in her head like hammer blows in time to the awful canned music.

"I'm going to see John on business . . .

"He's got a bull for me . . .

"I promised to go and look at it . . .

"How could I go till the hay was in? This weather won't last . . .

"It's not John's fête . . .

"You're not feeling ill, are you, Monica? Are you sure you're all right? . . .

"Then I don't understand . . .

"Working farmers don't go to fêtes . . .

"What am I supposed to do? Walk round looking stuffed?"

Monica handed over the coffee gateau. Her own words came back.

"I think you get out of these things on purpose."

'I still think so.' She visualised Juliet, gorgeous in the station wagon beside him.

"My God you're being stupid. Unfair as well." The back of his neck was scarlet.

Gently, Martin put out a finger and touched the sugar on top of a Victoria sponge.

"Don't be a little pig," Juliet said. "There's one for us in the tin."

At this point Mrs Webster appeared.

Monica had wanted to tear up her kitchen, her house, her

89

marriage, everything, and toss the pieces in the air.

"Here I am at last," Miss Henderson said. "You look done in. Go and have some tea, do dear. If you can get in. Every child in England is trying to eat ice cream."

"I don't want any tea," Monica said. "It's not worth the struggle."

In the circumstances Miss Henderson was more soothing than tea. She had never been anyone's mistress. She was fat and plain and her heart belonged to a fluorescent budgerigar.

Juliet found her way home by moonlight. The drive in front of her was striped with clear cut shadows. Somewhere a bird was singing and she thought 'That must be a nightingale. I've never heard one before.' Ahead, the drawingroom window was a yellow oblong. She let herself into the kitchen by the back door. On the table was a bowl covered with a saucer, and a note in Monica's handwriting "Chicken salad in fridge and cream for raspberries."

'The servant's night out,' Juliet thought, relieved at not being expected to make an appearance. She ate standing up, moving about, washing up and putting things away *passim*.

Gerald had said "Why not come and see my bull? You can't really want to go shopping."

She wanted to accept, with all the longing for shared activity induced by their lovemaking. But she said "You're crazy. I've got to go to the cinema."

"I suppose you ought to. What a pity."

Everything after the cornfield was an anti-climax.

The hall was in darkness. As she went past the drawing room door on her way upstairs she heard Gerald say "No bid." She hoped he would make some sign that he knew she was in the house, even if it was only to run his finger across her bedroom door or turn out the passage light while she was still in her bath. But when the bridge players came upstairs nothing happened. She lay awake a long time. It was disturbing to discover that she disliked the thought of another woman in his bed; that Monica was his wife and had a right to be there, made it more uncomfortable. Her last waking thought was 'I'd never stand life on the stud farm. I need a one girl man.'

12

The band of daylight lay across Juliet's floor from the door to her bed. Gerald walked along it carrying a cup of tea. Semi-darkness shrouded the rest of the room like the darkened wings of a stage.

The usual pleasure he took in meeting the conquered female and seeing his potency reflected in her eyes was enhanced by being able, this time, to come on her unguarded. Validated by a cup of tea he was invading her feminine privacy to wake her up. He picked his way carefully, to avoid disturbing her clothes on the floor. Sandals, bra, pants, frocks, lay where they'd dropped or been tossed on chairs. Make-up and bits of cottonwool, powder, letters, a glass of water, mixed haphazard on the dressingtable. Chaos which he would never have tolerated in wife or child, in Juliet he found appealing. So was her sleeping face.

"Juliet—" he lowered the cup on to her bedside table.

Juliet opened her eyes. She saw the cup of tea, his hand, a brown paisley silk sleeve, and she smiled. Then she met his eyes and felt kissed before she had been touched, with no bones left.

"I'm not going to kiss you now because if I did I'd want to go on and the children are already on their way." He went instead to draw the curtains.

'My body's out of control like a runaway horse. How odd to be like this for a man I don't know and don't perhaps even like,' Juliet thought, watching him walk towards the window. She saw his bare legs stepping over the nightie she'd discarded because of the heat. So he had no pyjamas on. 'I might be

93

waking up after a night in a hotel bedroom.'

"We seem to have skipped a stage," she said.

"A good thing too. It's time to get up, Juliet, it's Sunday, and you're giving Monica breakfast. She doesn't want it in bed, but she'd love it got for her. I've brought you tea to encourage you on your way."

Everything that passed between them was sexually charged. 'Too late to worry now,' she thought, enjoying her sensations.

"Watch that teacup! Here they come!" Gerald's eyes followed the line of her arm from her hand holding the cup to her bare shoulder and down the curve of her breast to the sheet.

"Juliet, Juliet, I won a coconut!" Martin jumped on the bed, snatched back the sheet and dived in.

Harriet leant against the bedside table. "He didn't really *win* the coconut. They let him get so close he practically touched it. Why have you got no nightie on?"

"Because I was too hot. Go and get dressed both of you. I've got to get breakfast this morning. No, Martin. Get out."

From the door, Gerald smiled.

'I'm a woman in a perspex box,' Monica thought, looking round the breakfast table. 'They can see me and I can see them but there's no proper communication. They hear what they think I'm saying. We meet, but we don't touch. What really goes on? They're obviously quite happy with each other. *They* know about *them*, but I'm cut off.

'I could drop right out.'

Monica watched, as if from her grave, the second wife caring for her children.

'She's quite sweet to them. They like her.' Juliet cut the top off Martin's egg and tucked a napkin under his chin. Gerald was smiling fondly. 'It's a family party. Poor ghost.

'All my day off is going to prove is that I'm not needed. Not wanted on voyage. Look at Gerald.'

94

His face was smooth as butter. His behaviour to Juliet was outwardly discreet, but to no purpose. Together they produced the atmosphere peculiar to newly married couples: that no one besides themselves exists.

"How was the film?" Monica asked, keeping to safe ground.

"Oh, one of those stark affairs where you're not sure what's happening except that it's nasty, and one thing dissolves into another. There was a huge breast that was terribly important, but I never quite made out why. It was quite restful. I more or less went to sleep."

"I want to go to the cinema," Harriet said. "Take us, Juliet. Please, please."

"You wouldn't like that film."

"Why not?"

"It had no proper story."

"X for sex," Gerald said. "They change the programme today, then it'll be the Beatrix Potter film. I'll take everyone to the cinema tomorrow afternoon and we'll have ice creams afterwards at Lucy Locket's. Now that's that, if you don't hurry we'll be late for church."

"Sit by me," Martin said, taking Juliet's hand.

"I'm not coming today. I'm going to do the chores, your mother's having a holiday. Come on children and I'll help you get ready."

'I'm too late to take her away from him now,' Monica thought. 'He sees nothing else. If I sent her away he'd call her back. He might want to keep her. I've got to sit it out.'

Juliet came downstairs with a child holding each hand. They hopped from step to step in their best sandals and white socks. The front door was open, a brilliant yellow oblong revealing hot sun out of doors. Side by side, Monica and Mrs Webster waited in the hall for Gerald to bring round the car. Both wore hats and carried gloves and prayerbooks. There was no

95

sap left in Mrs Webster's face while Monica's was still young and smooth, but otherwise, Juliet thought, they were branches off the same tree. 'They both subscribe to the same beliefs. They live by the same rules. They might be waiting for their carriage.' There was something so incongruous about Gerald's bare legs before breakfast, and his Sunday suit and wife and mother, that Juliet felt she was walking into a farce in which nothing need be taken seriously, or could be if she tried.

It seemed quite natural to her to make Monica's bed along with the rest, though she enjoyed, consciously, seeing inside the bedroom at last.

Monica, back from church, stood on the threshold trembling with rage. 'So she's been in here! The room's contaminated, it'll never be clean again.' It was as if she could see Juliet between these sheets. She put up her hands to take off her hat. 'How can I go on?'

Down on the terrace she lowered herself into the empty chair beside her mother-in-law. Today she had a servant. There was nothing whatever for her to do except watch Gerald. 'If only I could be certain!' she thought. 'He's had her. I *feel* sure. But how did it happen? And where? He did go and look at the bull, he described it to me last night. Gerald would call a bull Hercules. How quickly can you buy a bull? Did it take him five minutes or two hours? Was there time for both? Because he wasn't late home either, he was back soon after we were. I'm sure he dropped Juliet at the cinema, otherwise he'd never know what the programme was. Besides, she came back on the late bus, I heard her come in.'

There was no Sunday peace. Gerald kept darting into the kitchen: for ice, for lemons, for squash for the children. 'It would be better if Juliet was out here in full view and I was doing my usual conjuring. This week has seemed like a year.'

Finally Gerald said, "I'm going to winkle the cook out for

96

a drink."

Mrs Webster was watching him too.

Monica thought 'It's obvious even to his mother.'

Juliet was at the sink. Gerald pinned her arms from behind and kissed her ear.

"Don't!" she said. "Do be careful."

"No one can see."

"I daresay, but I'll break something."

"I'm sure you can leave everything now. Come and have a drink."

"I've still got to lay the table."

"I'll help you."

Outside on the terrace Monica and Mrs Webster listened to the noise of laughter and the tinkling of glass and cutlery that was coming from the diningroom. Gerald's voice floated through the window, warm and teasing.

'This afternoon I'll say something to him,' Monica thought. 'I'll screw up my courage.'

But Mrs Webster never left them alone.

"I don't think I'll rest," she said. "Such a waste of a lovely day. Then it's the last chance I'll have of seeing anything of Gerald. I must get back on Tuesday. No, Gerald, your accounts can wait till I've gone. It'll do you good to sit and do nothing for once."

Monica watched the children go off with Juliet, all three laden with picnic baskets. She waited in hope all the long afternoon till they returned. At one point she said "Do come and look at the rose garden, Gerald, I want to know what you think about it. What new kinds we ought to get."

But Mrs Webster got up from her chair and came too. For years she had kept an eye on Gerald's indiscretions, fearful of 'disgrace' when it meant scandal, and otherwise indulgent of 'success'. She was complacently aware that 'success' had now occurred; she read it in his face. Monica was not to be allowed to upset things. Mrs. Webster couldn't prevent her from monopolising Gerald in bed at night, but she intended to make sure there were no explanations by day. Her little plan was working out quite nicely.

She walked round the rosebeds. "That Josephine Bruce doesn't look very well," she said. "I'd have her out if I was you."

13

Juliet came down to dinner dreamy and golden from soaking up the sun, bringing with her the last of the hot day. She had withdrawn into herself, beyond the need to flirt, secure in being wanted. She was enjoying for the moment being unable to express her private relationship with Gerald. Her white frock was an unspoken signal that with the getting of this meal her responsibilities for the day were discharged. Everyone looked round as she came into the room. Conversation stopped.

To Monica she seemed molten with sensuality, sending out waves of sex so strong that it was quite indecent. Gerald was staring in open admiration.

Mrs Webster smiled, thinking how suitable Juliet would look in Monica's place.

"Well, Mother," Gerald said. "When are you off?"

"I told you Gerald. On Tuesday."

"We'll open a bottle of wine tonight and light the candles. Red or white? What's for dinner, Juliet?"

' "*Juliet?*" Am I here? Or am I not? Am I real?' Monica thought. "Red wine, Gerald," she said before Juliet could answer.

'It's like blood,' she thought, as Gerald filled her glass. 'Now I understand about the communion wine. This is my blood.'

"It's a pity Juliet doesn't play bridge," Mrs Webster said, seeing her as the new chatelaine. "You'll have to learn, dear."

"No, I don't think so. It's not for me."

'Bridge!' Monica thought. 'And I'm in torment.'

Gerald put a match to the candles. Their flames sprang up and shrank again to hug the wicks.

'Tonight I'll lie awake,' she decided, 'and think everything out in peace.'

The rattling curtain rings woke her from a deep dreamless sleep that left the night a blank and wiped out everything except the present moment. Sun poured in across her bed and lighting up the lining of the bed curtains bathed her in a rosy glow. Caught up in its radiance she watched Gerald crossing the room. She thought 'We're two halves of one person.'

"Your tea, darling," he said, kissing her.

She put her hand on his bare chest under his dressing gown. "Don't seduce me now. It's Monday, and Mother's champing for her tea."

At the word "Mother" memory came flooding back. She lay like lead, thinking while the sunlight dazzled her eyes 'I've been cheated of a whole night! I'm left behind, now I'll never catch up.' That piece of time had been taken away from her and destroyed. 'At least tomorrow Mother will be gone. I suppose that is something.' But she could hardly bear to get out of bed.

At breakfast Gerald said "If you're going shopping this morning you might get me a bag of cement. I could pick it up when we go to the cinema, but that would mean starting early."

The crumpled rug tossed on the back seat of the station wagon caught her eye; she folded it tidy and put her shopping basket down on top.

Behind Lucy Locket's bottle glass windows Monica and Lanthe sat opposite each other, tucked into high oak settles. Winter and summer a green underwater light shone inside the room. The sun never penetrated. Visitors found this quaint, but the locals, knowing the bottle glass was new, felt it was tiresome.

All the same, Lucy Locket was the only place to go because the cakes actually were home made and the cream real.

In silence they stirred their coffee round and round.

"Well, cheers," Ianthe said.

'What's the matter with her?' Monica thought. 'Is she uncomfortable because of the guilt she always has with me or is something else wrong? If only she knew, I'm the one who should be feeling guilty, I know far more about her than I ought.' Ianthe belonged to a golden age, when Gerald's infidelities had all been confided, serving only to enhance her own position as his wife.

"Cheers," Monica replied.

Ianthe emerging from her car in the market square had appeared at first as unlikely as a photograph. Then Monica's heart lifted. 'She might have been sent. As a saviour! Ianthe, of all people . . . We could easily have been at school together. Chums at that. Perhaps if I pretended we're both still sixteen and in the dorm we could manage a heart to heart.'

"Hi, Ianthe!" she said. "What happened to you on Saturday? You were about the only one"—'of them' she nearly added—"who wasn't there."

"Oh just children, as usual." Ianthe gave her big smile. "Caroline's got chickenpox. She's nearly out of her mind with itching, poor lamb. Monica! Super to see you. Let's have a coffee."

Ianthe's little round bottom was tightly outlined by her jeans. Thin straight sandy-coloured hair hung to her shoulders. People tended not to notice her eyes, what caught attention was her wide smiling mouth. She was one of those girls who look as if they'd been flung together and might at any moment come apart; her flesh spare but soft, her waist long and fragile. Even carrying a shopping basket her elbow bent backwards. No one would think that at school she'd been a junior county gymnast and now played squash and hunted as many days of the week as she could.

"How's Ray?" Monica said, putting off confidences.

"Terrified of getting chickenpox. He's so afraid it might stop him going to Sweden next month about a contract for his wretched machine tools that he won't go near the poor darling. Nanny's furious."

'It's really missing the Swedish blondes he's in a stew about,' thought Monica, 'and Lanthe's rolling up her sleeves already for the next row. I'm sure she knows I know. It seems stupid we can't mention it, in some ways our positions are so alike.

'But how can I compare my situation and hers when there's no comparison between Gerald and Ray?'

Ray was shoddy; he'd sold out to the worst in contemporary life, he regarded his cars as status symbols. He even looked flashy, with his hair too smooth and jackets too waisted; according to Gerald 'a bit of a bounder', and Mrs Webster's comment—just wrong, as usual—was 'not *quite*, dear.' Ray was undoubtedly a gent, it was his temperament not his birth that was off. If Lanthe hadn't been so goodnatured she would never have put up with him.

'What's really bothering her, I wonder? How on earth do I start?'

Monica's mind had become a creature in its own right, over which she had no control. She watched Lanthe's spoon going round and round inside the blue and green cup. Quite a pretty cup, but so thick the coffee cooled quickly. That was the worst of the local pottery.

'Something's new on her conscience. She's one of those reliable people who keep everything going; but I'm afraid not a saviour. More a good disciple. It's me that's being crucified. She won't notice either, why should she? She'd be any headmistress's choice for prefect, but never for head girl. Fated to become a pillar of the W.V.S. Me too, for that matter. We lead the same lives.'

Her pretence wasn't working, the situation refused to be contained in schoolgirl terms.

'If I don't make do with Lanthe there'll be no saviour.'

But all she could bring herself to say was "I'd forgotten you still had Nanny."

Why? It should have been so easy to talk to Lanthe, she was the most civilised of Gerald's mistresses and so pleasant. Her affair with Gerald had been quite jolly and left no emotional axes to grind.

Today Monica was obsessed and could only see Lanthe in her role as number 17 in the harem. Gerald had said of her that she carried an invisible hockey stick with her even between the sheets, "but I soon got rid of that". Poor Gerald! He had pulled out all the stops but didn't get much of a response.

How odd to be thinking this about Lanthe when they were sitting so close that their fingers on the table were almost touching. Their well-bred hands were kin.

"She nannies me as well," Lanthe said, "I can't think how you manage on your own."

"Both mine are at school now, I really get lots of time."

"And then of course you don't hunt."

Monica was seeing Lanthe and Gerald locked naked together like a Chinese puzzle, identical but opposite. Lanthe stood on one leg, the other supported under the thigh by Gerald's hand and hanging gracefully from the knee. One of her hands was round his neck, the other supported his opposite leg. Two figures on two legs only. Gerald was proud of this position, he'd got it out of a coffeetable book on Hindu sculpture. Lanthe was the only one so far who'd been able to manage it.

The pity of it was she was so lightly sexed. She'd been a sexual con too, according to Gerald, but so gymnastically fascinating and amusing it made up for it. The affair had come apart the minute Ray came home from abroad.

Inside her mind Monica put Ray into one pan of a pair of scales—the sort a stork flies about with on greetings telegrams—and Gerald in the other. Then she added Lanthe to Ray's side and herself to Gerald's. Gerald was much heavier because of all his mistresses. Ray had endless mistresses too, but they were washed away by Lanthe's rows and his grovelling repentance and toeing the line.

'Actually Lanthe's a much nicer character than I am. I couldn't bear it if Gerald toed the line, I'd be bored if he was faithful. We're both social pirates, me as much as him.'

Then it came to her, 'But if one pirate rats there is no court of appeal. If I lose my marriage I lose more than Lanthe would ever understand, something no other man except Gerald could ever give me.'

At the thought this might really happen Monica felt herself sweating.

"It's terribly hot in here today, isn't it?" she said.

"I suppose it is rather. How was the fête? Caroline was sick as mud at missing it."

"The usual bore, but the children loved it. Martin won a coconut. We took £300, which was good, considering."

How simple to be Lanthe and not care terribly much about sex. Gerald's variations had been hardly more to her than an interesting new way of doing Long Fly. Monica tried, and failed, to imagine what life would be like without this particular excitement. Not to care whether one had Gerald or not! She felt sick.

Lanthe looked at her with concern. "You've been overdoing it, overworking making cakes if I know you. If this heat's too much let's go."

"No. I'm all right. We've got Gerald's mother, you know what that's like."

Lanthe was not wearing a bra. Under her sweat shirt her small breasts looked as if they'd been pulled out like toffee and left with the nipples tilting upwards.

'And she's double-jointed, that's the thing, that's what smacked Gerald.'

At the tennis party where they first met Lanthe had shown off her suppleness by bending over backwards in an arc and turning herself into a hoop to pick up a tennis ball. In anyone else it would have been a blatant sexual gesture, but Lanthe was so innocent it would never occur to her she was poking her pubis in the eye of the world. Dimly Monica recognised that her own public fastidiousness covered up a deep concern for sex.

Gerald had stiffened like a pointer. Monica had seen him thinking instantly of all the possibilities.

'What a meaningless exchange this is we're having. I must talk to her, but I can't. I'm cut off. It's like shaking hands through prison barbed wire.'

Monica felt no weight pressing on the seat she was sitting on. Her legs were disconnected and her arms floated in front of her. The bottle glass windows were like the waves of the sea; the home-made fudge and cakes on display, groups of sea anemones and branches of coral. It frightened her to hear her voice coming out with the usual small talk while her mind remorselessly followed its own devices.

'I'm all in pieces. I'll never get out of here. I'll never feel sane again. Am I delirious, coming to after an operation?' Lanthe drifted in and out of reality, an attendant nurse.

'There's not going to be a saviour.'

Sadly Monica at last understood that just as she and Gerald were perfect partners in bed, so they had been partners in his pursuit of other women; and this made it impossible for her to have as a friend anyone who had been his mistress, because, in some sense, they had been her mistresses too. She had never seen this clearly before.

'But not Juliet. I know nothing about Juliet, I have no share in Juliet!' and this was a knife at her throat.

"More coffee, madam?" The waitress materialised, attentive beside Lanthe, who even in pink jeans was unmistakably county; Rachel would have had to stew and call.

At last Lanthe managed to say what was on her mind.

"Monica, there's something rather beastly happening. I think you ought to know. Rachel's telling everyone she saw your station wagon parked empty in Malthouse Lane with the labradors on guard—'just sex sentries' was what she said, she's beyond everything—when *you* said Gerald was going out on business. And half an hour before that she'd seen it whizz past the fête with Gerald and your au pair on board. You can imagine what she's making of it. I tried to shut her up, but it was like trying to stop the Flood. She's an odious woman."

So that was when.

"Shouldn't you say something to her?" Lanthe said gently.

"What's the use? Gerald had to go out on business and of course he gave Juliet a lift. But it's no good trying to explain to Rachel that farmers look at their corn. She wants it her way. If I take any notice people will think it's true. Rachel's too spiteful. No one will believe her."

But I do, she thought.

Lanthe was staring at her very oddly.

"Look Monica, I'm terribly sorry, I wish I'd held my tongue. You look all in, come and have a whisky."

"No thanks. I must get back." That's why the rug was crumpled. She was in a fever to get away.

The second self that had separated off—the unknown Monica who terrified her—and her conventional self, still trying to function on its own, shook hands to prevent her from speaking out to Lanthe. One part of her felt that she would be betraying her husband. The other was not going to be stopped. She wanted to examine the rug, then beat Gerald up and kill Juliet. She put down her cup with an unsteady hand and forgetting about the bill, hurried out of the door.

'I've failed,' Lanthe thought. 'I should have been able to

make her talk to me, but it's like trying to prize open an ice-berg. What she fails to see is that every woman in the place knows what Gerald's like and what he's after now. She's the only person putting up any pretence.'

When Monica drove out of town she was crying. She drove very fast. Well away from the village and Gerald's own land, where no one was likely to see her, she pulled in to the gateway of an empty field. With distate she picked up the rug and carried it through the gate.

"I'm sorry Gerald," she said, "but I've got to know, I can't go on."

She spread the rug out on the grass in the sun. Her eyes went straight to a small flat patch where the hairs were stuck together, glazed smooth instead of rough.

It was hot still noon. The birds were silent, resting, no creatures moved in the hedgerow. The engine in the distance she was listening to was her own heart beating. There was her proof. Having it made no difference at all one way or another.

For the moment Monica was quite calm, caught in the eye of the hurricane. All she felt was slight surprise that anyone so practised could be so careless. 'Poor Gerald. But then he's never tried to hide anything from me before.' It was like Martin trying to hide himself behind his hands.

14

As Juliet stepped out of the back door into the yard it seemed to her as if the sky had come down to meet the earth; she felt at one with Nausicaa going to spread the washing on the stones by the sea. With the basket of wet clothes hitched on her hip she made the journey out to the line in the field. Hot sun poured down, enveloping her bare arms and penetrating her dress to drench her skin. Fulfilled sex was making every physical activity, even domestic ones, primitively acceptable.

She put the heavy basket down on the grass, stretched voluptuously, and caught the line. Handling Gerald's shirts sent waves of desire through her body. Every shirt in turn said as she hung it up to dry "Now I've had you you can't escape, and there's more pleasure to come." She answered each of them "I could, but I don't want to."

'Turned into a handmaid,' she thought. 'But all this is just a game, I wouldn't do it for a man I meant to marry.' All this and Gerald too, was more like ancient Greece than the present day. He just put anything he fancied under his arm and ran off with it, like one of those stiff pricked figures running round a vase in a frieze. The wicker basket at her feet was bleached white with long use, and timeless. Up went his pants and a row of socks. She found a certain kick in being a handmaid, because she could stop whenever she chose. It came to her that he was like Odysseus too, an adventurer going through life from one woman to another with Penelope waiting in the background. He was two people inside one skin, a very odd mixture, the ancient Greek and a conventional British landowner. But the Nausicaa situation was reversed: he was at home, she was the wanderer.

She hoisted the washing line into the air on its prop and picked up the empty basket.

Monica had still not returned. In the kitchen Mrs Barden was ostentatiously mopping the floor round the washing machine. Juliet ignored the hostility that had been rampant all morning. "Mrs Barden," she said, "we don't want to drag Mrs Webster in from the garden. Ought we to do anything about lunch d'you think?"

"They usually have cold," Mrs Barden said. "On a Monday. Madam didn't mention it this morning."

"There's plenty of beef," Juliet opened the fridge, "and I could make salad and potatoes, but I'm not very good at puddings. We ate up all the raspberries yesterday."

"I could do them a chocolate blancmange. The children like that. You'll find the lettuces in the top left hand corner by the greenhouse."

"Why not take a basket and a knife?" But Juliet was already out of earshot. "These girls, they're all the same." Mrs Barden watched her crossing the yard. "It's his mother's fault. The old bitch. He's always worse when she's about. I did warn Mrs Gerald, I did my best. She should have sent that girl packing.

"Not that he wouldn't have found someone else. But under his own roof! It's not decent."

Her blood was still boiling from Rachel's remarks at the fête, aggravated by the gossip already flying round the village.

"That fat thing. Speaking to Mrs Gerald like that. A jumped up madam, no better than a tart herself. We all know what Mr Gerald's like, but she's got no call to say what she's saying, no one wants to see Mrs Gerald upset."

Juliet came back swinging a lettuce in each hand. Little bits of earth dropped on the clean floor and crumbled over the draining board. She unhooked Monica's apron and put it on.

Mrs Barden stared, her sense of fitness outraged. She opened her mouth and shut it again. Oh well, Mr Gerald's affairs were his own.

Out in the paddock Mrs Webster was determined to prove to Martin that his kite was not a white elephant. It was her last day and the children looked on with mixed feelings. The kite was a failure, but Granny could still be bled for treats. At the moment they were remembering that when she went away she always pressed tips into their hands, and they were unwilling to let her out of their sight.

Mrs Webster was running about in the tussocky grass while the kite hopped behind her, floating deceptively every now and then but unwilling to leave the ground. Her legs, clad in fine stockings and balanced on navy blue high heeled sandals, wove an erratic course between the anthills and thistles.

Harriet watched her grandmother with detached disquiet. Something awful was going to happen. It was stalking through the house, creeping up on her and she couldn't escape. Every day it came nearer. Granny was never going to make the kite fly. If she could have done everything would have been all right.

Harriet gave up and drifted off with Martin to look for plantains under the ha-ha.

Now she had finally lost the children's attention Mrs Webster happened on a thermal, and slowly, hesitating, the kite rose into the air as she pulled and let go, paying out the string.

"Look Martin! There you are! That's the way to do it! There it flies. Come and catch hold. Take this reel in your left hand. No, your *left* hand, Martin, and the string in the other. That's right. Now when you feel it really tugging you can let out a bit more string and it will go higher. You have to pay attention. You must keep it in the wind."

"There's no wind," Harriet said.

Martin stood tranced, feeling the pull of the kite that had suddenly turned into a huge bird miles up in the sky. But staring up at its fluttering tail he forgot all about the tension on the string, and the kite, losing the up current, came down like an arrow.

'Not good enough,' Harriet thought. 'Not to really work.' It had been a false flight and her unease remained.

Martin dropped the spool. "It's too difficult," he said. "Granny, if you can run, can't we play hide and seek?"

After looking at the rug for a long time, Monica bent down with difficulty and disgust, folded it, and put it in the back of the car. She drove back the way she had come and left it at the cleaners.

Mrs Webster said to Gerald "I don't think we should wait lunch, or we'll never be ready in time. As it's a cold meal it won't spoil. You can put Monica's on one side."

Halfway through her cold beef something made Juliet turn round. Quite silent, Monica was standing in the dining room doorway. Her face frightened Juliet, the eyes were dead like fish's eyes at the fishmonger's.

"What on earth happened to you?" Gerald said. "Have you been in an accident?"

"Mummy's got a headache, can't you *see*?" Harriet stated.

The scene in front of her didn't appear real to Monica. It belonged either to an old film she had seen in the past or to one that was going to happen in the future. The words came out of her mouth as if they knew what was expected of them.

"Your cement's in the back of the station wagon. I'm sorry I'm late. I met Lanthe. Then I forgot something and had to go back. I don't want lunch, I've got a shocking migraine. If you can supervise, Mother, I'll go and lie down."

"You do that thing, dear," and Mrs Webster smiled.

"You can't leave us to Granny," Martin said, and under the table, took Juliet's hand.

"But what about the cinema, Mummy?" Harriet was staring

with big eyes. "Will you be all right?"

"I shan't be coming, darling. Not feeling like this. It won't make any difference, Daddy will take you."

"Then I don't want to go. We can't go without Mummy, it's not fair! I won't leave Mummy!"

Monica put one hand up to her face. "Please don't shout. Don't get up Gerald, there's nothing I want.

"Tadpoles have to manage," she said as she walked away.

Watching Monica's face Juliet saw her mood change. From being a drowned woman, cold and still, she had come alive. Her eyes flickered and turned restlessly away, fixed on some alien purpose. 'What she wants is to be quit of us all so she can get on with whatever it is.' This frightened Juliet still more. She couldn't understand how Gerald could go on eating chocolate blancmange.

As soon as they were alone in the curiously intimate atmosphere engendered by clearing the table, she said to him "D'you think we ought to leave Monica? I don't believe she's got a headache, I think something's really the matter. D'you think she ought to be by herself?"

Gerald stared at her in astonishment.

"My dear girl why ever not? Don't look so worried, when Monica's like this all she wants is to be left alone. The kindest thing we can do is to remove Mother and the children so she can sleep it off in peace."

"I'll stay behind if you like."

"There's nothing whatever you could do. Be a Good Samaritan in the right direction. I'm not being left with Mother and a pair of sticky children on my hands."

"Well, if you're sure. All right. I suppose you know best."

"Yes, I do."

Juliet felt the invisible *No Trespassers* sign go up that Gerald sported where Monica was concerned. He was too close on the other side of the trolley for her to be able to think straight. She forgot about Monica.

Mrs Webster, too, understood that something was wrong. Who had Monica really met in town? Why was she pretending to have a headache? It must be Simon. A rendezvous when they were all gone! Her heart beat fast in pleasant anticipation of trouble as she got the children ready to go.

It was only Mrs Webster who found the outing a total success. For Juliet the afternoon was a dead loss. Gerald was abstracted, his face wore the expression of a man at an army parade. The cinema was hot and stuffy, the film a bore. She found herself sitting between Mrs Webster and Martin, and Martin had to be taken out in the middle to pee, trampling over innumerable feet. At his age did he go to the gents or the ladies? Harriet said: "This is a stupid film. That's not Mrs Tiggy Winkle, it's a person dressed up. I want to go home."

But Mrs Webster, with grisly gaiety, refused to give in, turning ice creams at Lucy Locket's into a full dress tea.

"It's my treat," she said, "for my last day. Besides it will save getting tea when we get back."

"On your head be it then, Mother," Gerald said.

'Your treat but no one else's,' Juliet thought, suffocated by Lucy Locket's antique gloom. 'If she crams any more into the children someone's going to be sick. Can't they see Martin's green already? Why doesn't Gerald stop it? What a way to take a girl out.'

Holding Martin's sweating head over the ditch on the way home she decided this was not her forte. It was a preview of a species of family life she had no intention of getting involved with. Back in the car Martin crawled on to her knee. Poor little Martin, he was too vulnerable. *He* didn't fit in with his grandmother either.

The happy picture on the back seat was not lost on Mrs Webster. Her hands folded lightly in her lap, she smiled ahead at the future. What a good augury! What a touching family scene!

"When we get home we won't disturb Mummy, will we?"

she said. "I'll put the children to bed while Daddy and Juliet get the supper. We'll have a bottle of wine, Gerald, and light the candles. As it's my last supper. And afterwards we can teach Juliet bridge. I'm sure she'll pick it up in no time. When I come again I'll expect to find you quite a good little player, dear."

'As if she was Christ,' Juliet thought. 'And I'm part of the fixtures and fittings I suppose.' Over his shoulder Gerald winked. 'No use winking. I'm not taking this at any price.'

Harriet's blood ran cold. What about Mummy? Granny's throwing her away. They were all soppy on Juliet. She pressed herself into the corner of the seat so that neither Martin nor Juliet could touch her and shut her eyes. When the car was safely moving she began an incantation under her breath, "Apple tree, apple tree, you've always listened to me. Please you must take Juliet away."

She repeated it over and over again.

15

"No I can't come, Monica. I've given you all the advice I can, if you won't send Juliet away or have it out with Gerald you'll have to lump it. Now do calm down like a good girl and get off the line, I'm busy."

"You're all shits. All of you." But Simon had rung off. Hot silence filled the bedroom. "Shit, shit," Monica said.

Gerald's smile hung in the air in front of her like the Cheshire Cat's grin. The other smiles she had left behind round the lunch table were only pink Guy Fawkes Day masks and she brushed them to one side. Not only would Gerald's smile not go, he grew round it till the whole man appeared to be there.

"You lied to me now you smile you lying bastard. Send Juliet away or else. If you don't get rid of her I'll kill myself."

Gerald said "I can't do that. I've never had a redhead before. Wonderful hair, red-gold. Have you seen her breasts?"

"Then you'll destroy our marriage. Do you understand, Gerald, you're tearing it up."

"It's only paper. Didn't you know?" He put his hand in his back trouser pocket and took out their marriage lines and under her eyes tore them up and tossed the bits in the air in a paper snowstorm. There were so many pieces, so small, flying in so many directions, coming thick and fast, she knew she would never be able to catch them all to put them together again. When the storm subsided Gerald had gone. His slippers poking out from under the bed were empty. She summoned him back.

"I've not finished, you can't go yet."

This time he was in his dressing gown, bare calves rose out of his slippers. No erection. The smile was still there.

"What are you doing with that?"

He was carrying a bottle. A green wine bottle. Claret. He said "It's high time the stopper was taken out," and pulled the cork.

"Stop," Monica said, "It's dangerous."

Smoke was coming out of the bottle and out of the smoke came a Genie, every moment growing huger. When the smoke dissolved Nanny's apron faced her and from above the white expanse Nanny's voice was saying "Monica stop playing with your toys and get off that pot. You can't sit there all day." In front of her a tall tower grew. She was building it step by step. Monica could still see how beautiful the coloured storeys were. One cup fitted on top of the next each step an ecstasy. She had just discovered how to do this and was about to put the last one in place.

A large pink hand came between her and the apron and swept the tower away.

She wanted to bite the hand but it was out of reach.

The pot stuck to her bottom, it came away with a suck. She held it with both hands and lifting it carefully emptied it over her head. Then she threw it on the floor.

"You disgusting child! Madam! Please will you come and speak to Miss Monica?"

Mummy appeared. Their shocked grown-up faces spoilt her beautiful rage. She was too frightened to cry. From that moment life was unsafe. There was a monster inside her too dangerous to let out.

"Gerald! Put back the cork," she said.

"I can't. I've thrown it away. In any case you know it's no good trying to re-cork bottles."

"You don't know what you're doing. I'm savage. I could tear you to pieces. You shouldn't have made me angry. You don't know what I'm like."

"Ah, but you don't know what I'm like," Gerald said, and his smile now was enigmatic. "Look."

"Gerald! Stop it."

"I'm no worse than you are."

He was coupling with Simon, giving her the cut direct as if she had been a garden party bore. Simon was smirking with his face painted as it had been when she first saw it.

"Simon get out of my place," she said.

"Go away Mummy, we don't want you," Simon said.

"He's nothing to do with you. It's Juliet he's in love with," she protested.

Little beads of cold sweat broke out all over her and wetted her clothes.

"I'm having hallucinations, I should've eaten lunch."

She was alone in the room, sitting on her bed, with her hand on the telephone. Gerald was not even in the house. He was in the cinema with Juliet.

She said "I can't share you with Juliet. Better dead."

Nothing moved. The curtains hung lifeless. Blue enamel filled the window frame.

"Not this window, the landing," she said, unwilling to watch herself walking to destruction in the dressingtable mirror.

At the top of the stairs she hesitated. The front door was held open and the sun lay arrogantly in a stripe across the hall. "There's no one there. The children must have left it unlatched," and she turned away down between the blank walls of the landing.

It was quite an effort to push up the bottom sash. She leant over the windowsill. It was a long way to fall to the hard stones. The fountain was hard too: glittering crystals thrown into the air and frozen there. Not moving at all. Frightened she tried to conjure up Gerald to witness what she was about to do, but the smile didn't come back and no matter how closely she looked she could see neither herself lying smashed nor Gerald in tears beside her, only the hard flagstones, quite bare. There was no one but herself, trying to pluck up courage to climb on to the windowsill and let go.

Tears of rage came into her own eyes. "I'll haunt you for this," she said, "every night of your life, I'll stand by the bed and wail till you sweat with fear."

"Don't you believe it," Gerald said on the warm air. "I shan't notice you. I'll have Juliet in my arms, she'll comfort me. She'll be my wife instead."

When they're not making love he'll tell her about his other women. He'll talk to her about me.

Such pain pierced Monica at the thought of Gerald talking about her to someone else instead of to her about them that she stopped in her tracks.

"Don't you think you will ever have another wife," she said and lowered the sash.

She felt quite calm now. Incomplete, imperfect, it was neither here nor there and didn't matter, Gerald belonged to her only, no one else should have him. As she turned her back on the window she heard the fountain playing again.

Beside her in the cut glass bowl the roses shed their petals in a drift across the table, leaving bare starfish centres.

"You'll have to wait," Monica said. "Now I *have* got a migraine."

Her feet were taking her away to oblivion, her open bedroom door welcomed her in, the harts, leaping so statically across the bed curtains filled her with gratitude. She shed her clothes. How deep the pillow was. How smooth the linen sheets, slippery with a hundred years of use, the embroidered Webster monogram denying follies. They were all whispering to her: "If you are in the bed there's no room for her."

16

Mrs Webster had brought the business of arrival and departure to a fine art. Her departures were the more dreaded by the family, giving scope as they did for maximum uncertainty. All the faces round the breakfast table were strained. Monica in addition felt a total sense of unreality. Perhaps after they'd seen Mother off the premises it might lift. Mrs Webster had come down to breakfast with her hat on and this at least signalled an intention to go. Monica stared in unbelief at the nest of false navy blue petals on her mother-in-law's head.

"You look pale, dear. Are you sure you feel quite well? If you're not the thing I can stay another day and put you back to bed."

"I'm perfectly all right, Mother."

"Can we come with you to the station, Granny?"

"We'll see. Now. Who is going to take me? Daddy came to fetch me, so it should be Mummy's turn."

"John's bringing the bull this morning," Gerald said. "I ought really to be here when he comes."

"Of course if Monica isn't feeling fit she shouldn't drive the car. You mustn't let her, Gerald. I'll ring the hotel and say I'm staying on."

"I'm quite fit, thank you, Mother. If you children are going with Granny you'd better wash. Gerald. Couldn't John come this afternoon?"

Juliet put down her coffee unfinished. As she left the room she caught Monica's eye and was shocked by the despair she read there. "Sorry I can't drive," she said, and escaped upstairs, thinking: 'None of this is my business, I'm only here for six weeks.' But her own personal drama was not comfortable either. 'I hope Oliver gets sunburn. I hope Lucy peels.'

'*I am so very fond of pleasure*
That I cannot be a nun,'

she quoted and went to make the beds.

She was upstairs in the best spare bedroom, collecting Mrs Webster's discarded linen, when Gerald came in, picked her up and laid her on the bed.

"I've always wanted to make love in this room," he remarked, "it used to be my nursery."

Sun poured in on them through the open window.

"I need two wives, I'd like to give you a baby. Don't go away."

Mrs Barden had spent a frustrating half hour putting two and two together. Now at last she stood in the doorway, looking for traces of goings on. But the bed had been reconstituted and on the flounced cretonne cover there was not a dent or a wrinkle to be seen: all sign of habitation had gone, even the smell of Eastbourne had disappeared; the window had been pushed up as far as it would go and the curtains stirred gently in the light morning airs.

She moved slowly in, picked up the biscuit box from the bedside table and with a sigh, pocketed the tip Mrs Webster had left underneath. Worry for nothing. That girl hadn't got there first. Of course *she* wouldn't know Mrs Webster's ways, always trying to make people do extra, the old cow. Mrs Barden flicked the bedside table with her duster, lifted the bed cover, scrutinised the pillow. No blonde hairs there. No matter, goings on she was sure there had been. What else would Mr Gerald have been doing, coming out of here so pleased with himself and shutting the door behind him? Not letting her in to clean, as she had been about to; carting her off with him down the passage. ' "Oh Mrs Barden, the very person I wanted. You can come along and help me turn our mattress, it takes two pairs of hands." Turn that mattress indeed! You know quite well it never has been turned yet, it's not the sort that *needs* turning, you was just trying to keep me out of here. Giving the girl a chance to tidy up. You can't pull the wool over *my* eyes, Mr Gerald, and if you make a habit of having that Juliet under this roof there's going to be trouble.'

She wondered whether to speak to Monica. But before the hoover started its whine she concluded: better to let Mrs Monica soldier on in ignorance.

Downstairs in the kitchen Juliet said to Gerald "You do take the most appalling risks. Mrs Barden's bound to smell a rat."

"It doesn't matter how big a rat she smells as long as she doesn't see it."

Laughing, Juliet shuffled Mrs Webster's sheets into the washing machine.

The nearer Monica got to home the more afraid she grew that she had been away too long.

"No, children, I'm not going to take you shopping this morning. If you don't stop being a nuisance I'll put you out of the car and you can walk down the drive."

And why was Gerald on the doorstep?—Indecently debonair, and far smoother than he had any business to be simply because his mother had gone.

Had he or hadn't he?

In which bed?

She forgot about putting away the car, pulled up and got out, her eyes blazing, her cheeks pink with rage.

"You utter shit," she said, "landing me with Mother. She was impossible. You did it on purpose."

"Little pitchers, darling. You ought to get angry more often, it suits you."

How could he look at her like that if he had? No trace of guilt. Good symptom or bad? It could be either. If he *had* and managed not to look guilty, things were even worse than she had imagined.

"Daddy. The train nearly left Granny behind."

"Don't be silly," Harriet said. "It couldn't go, the carriage door was still open. *I'm* going to put my 50p in my piggy bank."

"So you got your graft. Now clear off both of you and find Juliet."

"Where is she?"

"I should try the kitchen. Use your intelligence."

"I'm not forgiving you," Monica said. "Why aren't you out on the farm? I don't believe John's coming at all. You could perfectly well have gone yourself."

To prolong the moment the better to decipher Gerald's mood, hoping for some sign that would give him away, she drew out the story of Mrs Webster's departure.

"She got in and out like a yo-yo, the porter must've arranged the cases a dozen times, I thought the children'd go hysterical. Would you believe it? She only tipped everyone when the carriage actually began to move. Then we had the waving nonsense."

Monica had been pinned to the platform till Mrs Webster finally disappeared and the window was no more than a snakescale on the train.

"Of course after that the children wanted to go shopping."

All in vain. Gerald's face was entirely filled with desire for herself, a barrier which made it useless for her to go on.

"Here *is* John," he said. "Come along old girl, we'll go and admire Hercules."

"You're not at all sorry, are you? Wait for me while I just see about lunch." She was sure that if only she could look at Juliet she would know.

But Juliet, pouring out milk for the children, was neither more nor less radiantly sexual than she had been for the last ten days.

'I'm going mad,' Monica thought, 'they hadn't a chance. It's Mrs Barden's day for the bedrooms. John's here.' Perhaps there was no need to worry, perhaps her agony was all for nothing. There was no way of checking now, she had destroyed any evidence. The rug was going round and round in the big drum at Kepe Klene.

As the train carried her towards Eastbourne a series of charming vignettes flashed through Mrs Webster's mind—Gerald and Juliet in last night's candlelight. The look in his eyes was not that he reserved for his usual women, it quite took her back to his early courting days—Gerald and Juliet kneeling at the altar in the parish church. The family veil would look well on her blond hair, and of course she would have no heirloom of her own to wear. Martin in a proper school cap, being turned at last into a proper Webster and a gentleman with the help of Mr Peters.

She began once more to permute the rooms in the Dower House to suit their new functions.

17

With Mrs Webster out of the way it was as if a weight had been lifted from everyone's head. A feeling of leisure and holiday seeped into the atmosphere, the air inside the Hall was less oppressive; Juliet found herself running her hand down the banister rail with love. She was wearing dark glasses and carrying her bath towel. The children, freed from their grandmother's censorship, ran in front of her barefoot, wearing their oldest, most exiguous shorts. They were making for the paradise below the ha-ha and an afternoon left to their own devices.

Gerald and Monica stood on the terrace arm in arm.

"Isn't it marvellous to have the place to ourselves again?" Gerald said. "Since we've got a slave I'm going to take you out to dinner to celebrate. It's time we had an evening on our own."

The warmth in his voice was genuine. Monica had to believe him. With wild hope she wondered if perhaps the whole of the last fortnight had been a hallucination induced by his mother. It was almost as if he had forgotten Juliet.

Up the yew walk Martin was advancing slowly, absorbed in a private world. He was stark naked and oblivious of his parents' presence. On the edge of the fountain's basin he straddled his legs and taking deliberate aim peed in a wide arc to meet the rising jet.

"Good boy," Gerald said smugly.

"I don't understand you. You let him pee, but you won't let either of them bathe."

"Harriet bullies him. He's asserting himself. Girls can't pee like that poor things, they don't know what a splendid feeling they're missing. Don't tick him off he's happy."

"You've seen too much of Hercules. You've got virility on the brain. What's Juliet doing I wonder, letting him loose like that?"

"She's in a state of nature too I suspect."

The silence grew heavy between them. Gerald appeared to be absorbed in shifting a small piece of grit with his toe towards the line between two paving stones. The grit became of the utmost importance to Monica. The whole future depended on whether or not it crossed the line. He's going to tell me, she thought, everything's all right. The grit reached the crack and stuck there. Gerald's foot lost interest in its task.

"I'm sorry about Mother," he said. "You've had too much of her this time. It's been my fault, I'll try not to let it happen again. Anyway now she's gone and tonight we'll enjoy ourselves. I've got to go in to pick up a drench for one of the cows, I'll book a table at the White Lion." He put his arm round her waist. "You make the necessary domestic arrangements darling. There's nothing you want while I'm about it, is there?"

Only the truth, she thought. Gerald's arm was no more comfort than an iron railing behind her back.

Above the ha-ha Juliet and Harriet, naked as Gerald supposed, lay on the towel side by side.

"I must get rid of these white bits," Juliet said. "If anyone comes I can always roll myself up. You don't need to bother. Why don't you run about with Martin?"

"I like it here. Soon I'll have breasts. Look." She sat up, pointing to the nipples on her flat chest. "Can I try your lipstick?"

"If you like. But it's in my room."

"I don't mind. Where?"

"On the dressingtable. Bring it here and I'll do it for you."

"No, I can myself."

Harriet had affairs of her own to attend to. Seizing her

chance, with even Martin otherwise occupied, she drifted away across the lawn. Gerald's arm, she noticed, was round Monica's waist. She didn't believe in it. Unseen, she escaped through the walled garden to the orchard. In order to make the connection between the apple tree and Juliet she needed a leaf to put in Juliet's bed. She asked for help as she picked it, and to make sure of being heard, changed the dirty water in the jam jar and filled it with fresh flowers. She felt the magic stretching like a single silken spider's thread between the leaf in her hand and the tree.

Which was the best place? Not under the pillow, between the sheets where Juliet would have to touch it. When she had finished the bed looked so smooth no one would ever guess the cover had been disturbed.

The muddle on Juliet's dressingtable made it difficult to find anything. Harriet's eyes focused on the little card of contraceptive pills. "Don't touch," rang in her ears, but curiosity, and an intuition as to what they were, were too strong and her fingers picked it up before she knew what they were doing. The white pills frightened her with their concrete suggestion of danger, they were like little bombs, she wanted to steal them and bury them in the garden where they could do no harm. Then nothing could happen. But suppose it did? She imagined Juliet fat with a baby that half belonged and could push her out. She breathed on the pills, hoping her breath would make Juliet sick, and put them back.

Her hand moved on, picking up one object after another and putting it down again in a slightly different place while she told it that it wasn't wanted here, it was time for it to go. When it was the lipstick's turn she painted her mouth. She held her lips stiffly apart because of the thick feel and walked like a priestess to rejoin Juliet in the sun.

"Not bad at all," Juliet said.

Gerald went indoors quite confident he had everything satis-factorily sewn up, he was so sure of Juliet at this point that he could afford to put her aside for one evening. Deep in his soul he knew she was something that he had to have, like bread, and because he couldn't bear the idea of her not being available, in fancy she was already Wife Number Two. Every member of his household had a proper function: it was only right that the junior wife should run about after Monica, as part of his establishment Juliet would have to pull her weight.

Having picked up the medicine he crossed the Market Square, an extra swagger in his walk. Outside the White Lion the sight of Lanthe, who had been a wholly creditable episode, bolstered his ego still further.

"What are you doing here?" he said. "Come and have a drink."

"You're a life-saver. It's Caroline's spots, she's madly itchy. I've got to collect dope for her at the surgery. Poor lamb she can hardly bear herself; didn't Monica tell you?"

"No, but we've had Mother and you know what that's like. She went off this morning thank God. How's Ray these days?"

"Awful. Like a bear with a sore head. I do wish he'd be more of a father to Caroline. He won't go and see her because of her spots. He goes on as if they were my fault."

"Don't stand for it, tick him off. He's an awful moral coward, if you go for him and tell him he's the world's worst father he'll cave in. Make him play ludo with her."

"You know how he is. He's supposed to be going to Sweden. He's terrified of missing all those lovely blondes if he catches spots himself."

"He's not so bloody marvellous—what makes him think they're waiting for him? Up the Home Counties."

"British is best?"

"Well, yes. No need to go out of this country."

"Gerald, you cheer me up."

"Mind you don't let him off."

Lanthe fiddled with her glass, playing trains on the mahogany.

"Gerald. What's the matter with Monica? I thought yesterday she seemed a bit het up."

"Oh? D'you think so? I haven't noticed anything, she seems all right to me. Mother always takes it out of her and this time has been worse than usual. She'll be all right now. That reminds me, I must book a table. We're celebrating tonight."

From experience Lanthe knew exactly what stage his infidelity had reached. It was not his Mother's departure he was celebrating. He was crowing on his dunghill. This was the honeymoon period; in due course diminuendo would set in.

After a second whisky she plucked up enough courage to say "You don't suppose Monica's a bit jealous?"

"Whatever makes you imagine that? Good God, are you mad, Lanthe? You know she knows my form."

"Sorry. Don't be cross."

Gerald put his hand on her knee. "You mustn't let Ray get you down. Find a distraction."

In full fig Gerald and Monica swept down the stairs and out to dinner without a backward glance, leaving the number of the White Lion by the telephone as if Juliet had been Mrs Barden and loth to look it up in the book.

"Take care my lad, you're not God," Juliet said to his retreating dinnerjacket. But beyond telling herself that he was the bottom and the end she couldn't be bothered to pick holes. What sense in tearing the wings off the joy as it flies?

The sun was still coming into the house as it had done upstairs this morning, merely looking through a different window. It fell on her as she ate her supper at the kitchen table, bathing her in light, making a miniature of itself in every saucepan on the stove, and she sat on, unwilling to leave it behind. Not that the house was unfriendly, rather the reverse, but it had developed a life of its own, and she was reluctant to sit in the drawing room where she felt overlooked by the formal furniture, or worse still, the diningroom, where that galaxy of Mrs Websters commented from the walls. Accompanied by the tick of the grandfather clock she went up to bed.

Monica, in defiance of Mrs Webster, to prove the rose was perfectly well, had re-filled the bowl on the landing with Josephine Bruce. The deep velvet blooms glowed nearly black in the half-light and drew Juliet to the window to bury her face in their petals. Her hair fell round them, their scent anaesthetised her. 'Why stay outside? Why not give in?' she thought and was overcome by the panic of an animal walking into a snare. If she let herself go, if she got too involved with Gerald, the house itself would trap her and tame her as it had trapped and tamed other women in its day. In this warm scented alcove where other ages outweighed the present she felt herself assessed and passed as a perfect candidate for the Webster gallery.

"You're wrong," she said, "I belong elsewhere," and she hurried to the safe disorder of her room and deliberately began to think about Oliver.

The chaos of her dressingtable was subtly different. Like most untidy people Juliet noticed the smallest shift in her own strew at once. That little demon Harriet, of course. Suddenly uneasy, she checked the card of pills, but none were missing. With a slight qualm of guilt she put the card away in a drawer.

Outside the colours began to disappear; no man-made noises disturbed the night. Against the distant murmur of falling water her thoughts unfolded one by one in her mind like flowers opening. Oliver's eyes had the quality of nightfall. He was bound to discover how tiresome Lucy was, through all those hot miles. And surely a bore in bed. Every person was divided into compartments: nice or nasty, clever or stupid, plain or good-looking, sexy or cold, the segments fitting together like marestail grass to make a total that was desirable or the reverse. As she was discovering, sexual skill could exist on its own and needed an independent box. A man could be a star performer like Gerald and yet fail to come off in the round. With complete certainty Juliet knew she could have him if she wanted; it appeared to her that she could take him away from Monica any time she liked.

"But I don't like. Out of bed I'd be bored."

Now the moon was rising above the trees, a lop-sided moon, just over half full, changing outlines, producing them transposed in black and silver, air and matter interchanged. The moonlight transformed the landscape outside and the room around her so that the two fused together and Juliet, crossing the floor to her bed, felt she was walking through water. Sexual power flowed through her. Poor Gerald, by opening her eyes he was digging his own grave. "I can have who I want when I want," she thought: and climbed into bed. Her foot encountered the apple-leaf and fished it out. It lay on the sheet, black in the moonlight. Its presence was disturbingly hostile. She wondered why. And how had it come there?

Monica knew the pattern of these celebratory dinners of Gerald's by heart. They always took place at the White Lion with champagne accompaniment, and sooner rather than later he came across with an intimate description of the defects of the outgoing incumbent: Rachel's banal privates, Anne's tiny breasts, poor Betty's tendency to go limp, Annabel's low slung bottom. The evening always ended up in bed behind the tapestry curtains, where he proved to Monica every time that she was the only woman who could hold him. Tonight there was a new edge on her anticipation. It added to her pleasure that while Gerald was behaving to her as if no other woman existed, Juliet should be left behind where an au pair belonged: in the kitchen; but at the same time she was mortally afraid that something was going to go wrong. She was waiting for one thing only: the moment when Gerald began pulling Juliet to pieces, tearing her limb from limb as a sexual object and a human being; laying every defect bare. Monica knew that till she heard him talk like that she would never be happy on earth again.

As the waiter pulled out a chair for her she said,

"Let's have lots of champagne."

Gerald said "Mother wants to come back to the Dower House but I've headed her off. I've been thinking, I don't want the children to go away to school. What have you heard about the Grammar? John says his boy's doing very well there."

"Martin would hate grammar school."

"I don't believe he would you know. And if Mother thinks she can get a son of mine sent to Eton she's got another think coming."

'*Mother*!' Monica thought. 'I could strangle that woman. She gets in the way even when she's not here.'

She drained her glass and held it out. Her surroundings were losing their charm. The diningroom was too familiar, the pink lighting stale. She was in a sort of limbo, the evening was like an old photograph, out of focus and beginning to brown at the edges. Instead of talking about Juliet, Gerald entertained her with an account of Lanthe's troubles.

"The man's not adult," he said. "He's like a small boy who thinks he can eat a ton of ice cream. Quantity's all he understands, he's got no discrimination at all. He'd be happy with a rubber doll if it was blonde and said yes."

"Poor everyone."

Lanthe was stale past history. 'I'm like a vampire,' Monica thought, 'wanting fresh blood.' "Give me some more champagne, Gerald," she said. 'I'm shut out of his whore house. It's the first time he's done it.' She was terribly afraid.

It astonished her that he didn't see how this sexual mass was turning into a black one. The ritual had gone wrong, no breaking of bread was taking place, no tearing of Juliet apart as the service ordained.

What was the point of this dinner? Still no Juliet. Talk, Gerald. You can't get off with hush money.

Rage that had been boiling through her veins for days was getting out of hand. The Furies standing behind her chair smiled. She felt their presence and trembled. Meanwhile the champagne was getting in the way, falsifying her reactions, and she was overcome by a maudlin pity for Gerald, herself, the whole world. A rosy cocoon of sentiment laced with sex wrapped her up, and in view of the light in Gerald's eye she found this soothing, until, as they came out of the White Lion, the fresh air hit her like a sledge hammer. At once she was drunk. Then she realised her period had begun. She was moving further into the dark.

"Shit, I'm done for," she said.

"What on earth do you mean? Darling, you're as tight as a tick."

"I've got the curse. That's fate all over. It might've held off till tomorrow."

"My poor sweet, bad luck."

"I forgot the date." To screen herself from Juliet she presented the wrong enemy: "It's your mother's rotten fault."

As she wove across the hall Gerald took her arm. "Watch it, or you'll come a cropper. I shouldn't have let you have all that champagne."

"Carry me."

"Not upstairs, old lady. Catch hold of the banisters and I'll push. You haven't got a pain, have you?"

"Not a pain. Just drunk, how shaming."

The concern in his face struck her as overdone. Bad luck! Not for *you*, it isn't. You're let off, aren't you? *I* know—afraid your cock wasn't going to come up to scratch. Too much Juliet this morning. You *did* have her.

"Fuck everything and if you laugh Gerald I'll kill you." She lifted her arms for him to peel off her dress. *Men were*

135

deceivers ever. But not Gerald to me, impossible. Tears of self-pity rose in her eyes. She searched his face that was coming and going like the Cheshire Cat, for signs of deceit, for an inch of smile, but could detect none. She was too drunk, gave up, crawled into bed, and passed out before she even knew whether he got in beside her.

18

To Monica, living perpetually with suspicion, the heat day after day grew increasingly oppressive; there was too much of it. It made things too easy for Gerald to do as he pleased. The détente caused by Mrs Webster's going developed into a general loosening of moral fibre that was disturbing, the elastic had stretched so far there was no bracing it again. Control slid out of her hands.

Harriet came into the kitchen without her clothes.

"What on earth are you doing like that?"

"Losing my white patches. Juliet says I don't need clothes yet. Not in the garden."

"You'll shock Mrs Barden. And you can't go out on the farm like that. The men won't understand. I don't care what Juliet says. Go and put on some shorts at once."

"What's wrong with my bottom half?" Harriet gave Monica a sideways look.

"Nothing at all. It's a very nice bottom half, but you know perfectly well most people feel shy about nakedness and you don't want to hurt their feelings. Go and do as you're told."

Juliet indeed! And where was Gerald? This is intolerable, she thought, I'm watching all the time. But I can't keep my eye on them every minute of the day. In this weather he can have her anywhere any time he likes. Under a hedge.

They both radiated sexual activity. It was quite embarrassing to be with them at meals.

Harriet drifted in again. "Is *this* better?"

Monica thought of harnessing her as a spy. Shocked at herself she said "That's fine. What's Martin doing?"

"I don't know. Fishing I think."

"By himself?"

"I think so."

"Why isn't Juliet with him? He might fall in."

"Fall *in*? *Martin*?" Harriet stared at her mother. "Martin can *swim*, Mummy."

"Where *is* Juliet?"

"Helping Daddy wash the car. I'm going out."

Harriet circled the station wagon like a dog inspecting an intruder. Neither Juliet nor Gerald took any notice. She left them and went off to the pond.

"Juliet's going," she said to Martin.

"No she's not. She hasn't told me."

Harriet noted with satisfaction that the rod quivered.

"She is. I can make her."

"You can't."

"I can."

"You can't."

"I can I can I can," Harriet chanted, marching back towards the house.

"You can't!" Martin shouted, running after her, the fishing line trailing, catching in the grass, breaking, losing the hook.

"Can."

"Can't. I hate you."

"Stop it at once." Monica came out into the yard. "What on earth is all this about?"

Martin burst into tears. "She made me break my line."

On the other side of the yard Juliet and Gerald, one each side of the station wagon, leant their elbows on the bonnet, deep in conversation.

Monica thought, didn't he *hear* the children? He's not cleaned that car in a thousand years, what's he up to now?

Once more it was Juliet's afternoon off. They're going to go away, she decided in anguish. He'll take her to the bus and I shan't see him again. They're cleaning the car to elope in.

138

But when the time came Juliet walked up the drive and caught the bus by herself. Like most people in the grip of sexual passion she felt no need to consult anybody's feeling except her own. In any case her moral sense was satisfied because she didn't intend to steal Gerald for ever. The hot sunny days dropped in front of her one after the other, each a separate offering to be enjoyed for itself. Her encounters with Gerald, planned or unplanned, she took as they came, living in the moment, unworried. The prospect of an afternoon on her own was quite welcome.

"Now," Gerald said. "What does everyone want to do? Children, let's have it."

"Swim," they said.

"Right. It's so hot I'll bend the rules, you can play in the fountain. What about it? Who'll turn it up?"

Monica's relief that Gerald was still with her was almost worse than knowing she had lost him. The cat and mouse situation went on. He's too happy, she thought. If life was normal he'd never let them do that.

But in spite of herself, she enjoyed sitting with him in the sun; listening to the children's voices she relaxed. Gerald was so much himself that slowly, like the outgoing tide, the nightmare receded and, as in the aftermath of migraine, just the present moment was real; precious and without pain.

The afternoon stretched peacefully into evening. The children had their baths and Gerald read them bedtime stories. Then he joined Monica and they changed for dinner together and ate their meal companionably at the dining room table, as if such a thing as an au pair had never entered their lives.

"I think the weather's going to break," Gerald said. "I missed the forecast but I smell thunder. A good thing the hay's all in."

"We could do with a storm. The garden's parched, if we don't have rain soon I shall lose my beans."

Monica felt a storm would be the answer to prayer. It would

rain Juliet off.

Afterwards they sat one each side of the fireplace in the drawing room, Gerald with the *Farmer's Weekly*, Monica with her tapestry. For the first time for days she sorted out the wools, matching the colours with pleasure against the design.

But the telephone rang and with foreboding Monica put down her needle.

"I'll go," Gerald sprang to the door. When he came back his face was a map of distaste.

"It's for you. Your tame queer wants to speak to you."

At that moment Monica hated him. She wanted to scream "You're rude about my friends, you don't want me to have any, and you expect me to put up with your concubine under this roof." But she had a better way of hurting him:

"I've asked Simon to come to drinks on Sunday," she said when she came back.

"What?"

"He wanted us to go to him, he was hoping to see Mother," she lied. Simon had been apologising for his bad behaviour to her, excusing himself with deadlines.

"You know I don't want him in the house."

"That's all very well, but he *is* my friend and we've been too rude for too long. In any case it'll be fun for Juliet." She chose her insult carefully. "I expect she's one of his fans."

Gerald's face flushed with rage, she had succeeded in making him really angry for once. He put down his paper with exaggerated care and began to walk towards the door.

There was an iron curtain of lies between them. Unable to bear it any longer Monica made up her mind to speak. Each step he took made it harder. The words were ready in her mind: "I know you're lying to me. You've had her. Please don't go on pretending."

But by the time she managed to open her mouth the door was shutting behind him.

In the hall the telephone rang again.

Gerald put his head round the door. "That was Juliet," he said coldly. "She's missed the last bus. We can't let her take a taxi all that way, I'll have to go and fetch her."

"I suppose you must."

Monica looked at the clock. If he drove fast they should be back again in an hour and a quarter. Allow quarter of an hour for contingencies. If they're later than an hour and a half I'll know they've been making love."

The embroidery lay untouched in her lap. She watched the minutes on the clock face pass.

Outside the telephone box in the village Gerald stopped the car. Juliet had not missed the bus, their meeting was pre-arranged.

"Get in," he said.

"We really ought to be more careful. Someone's sure to notice."

"What if they do? No girl should walk up our drive alone at night. Not these days, not with all the things they say in the papers."

"I hate lying to Monica."

"You haven't lied to her. All you've got to do is go on saying nothing."

"But that *is* lying, really."

"Oh rubbish."

"Where are you going?"

"Just up the drive."

"Gerald. I won't be made love to in the car."

"What an idiotic suggestion. What d'you take me for?"

When he stopped the car and turned off the lights Juliet was nearly blinded.

"Take my hand," he said.

"Where are we going now?"

"By the pond, under the oak tree. Where the children fish."

This time there was no rug. Under the oak tree the grass was dry, short but soft, the turf was as ancient as the turf under the yews. Gerald made love to her as beautifully as ever and for a moment Juliet forgot everything else.

The sky had already clouded over. There were no stars, no moon, the night wrapped them up, confining them to an island bounded by touch. On the pond a moorhen made its harsh remark.

"I've always loved this place. When I was a boy I used to lie here for hours watching the birds," Gerald said, and it occurred to Juliet that with his lovemaking he was performing a series of fertility rites, consecrating the sites important to him; first the cornfield, then his nursery, now this.

"Don't ever go away. Change your name by deed poll. I can keep you, there's plenty of room."

"Gerald, you're crazy. Do shut up, you're distracting me."

"You must learn to talk and make love at the same time, it adds to the pleasure." But the usual conviction was missing. Though she couldn't see his face Juliet felt sure he was thinking of something else. They had never made love in the dark before, but she found she could tell from the feel of his body.

"It's like crumbs in bed," she said. "When you go on about technique it makes me feel it's you, not me, you really care about."

"There you're wrong. Juliet, I'm quite serious; stay. I'd like to give you a baby."

"Listen—I don't want a baby just now. I've got a degree to take and a whole other life. Besides, Monica would hate it. Have you thought about that? It's a mad idea."

"You don't know anything about her. Leave that to me."

"I see, keep off the grass. Poor No. 2 Wife, no place in the nest."

"Don't joke." He sounded huffy. "Monica wouldn't mind, I can make you both happy, I could manage two wives. I always satisfy my women, don't I now? Admit it."

"All right, leave Monica out of it, but what about me? Perhaps *I'd* mind. Sometimes I think you're only intelligent

142

with your prick."

Gerald's hand stopped its caressing. "It's a very good thing to be intelligent with. *For Pistol's cock is up and flashing fire will follow* . . . Juliet I'm in dead earnest. Please never go away."

"I'm serious too. I'm not the sharing type. I've explained, I *can't* stay."

"Don't have such a bourgeois attitude. Juliet darling, I've got plenty of money, there's no reason at all why I shouldn't make you my common law wife. I'll talk to Monica about it tonight."

"Please do no such thing or I'll go tomorrow. You mustn't say *anything* to Monica because I have absolutely no intention of changing my mind. For one thing, I'm not in love with you."

"But you ought to be."

"I believe you mean that."

"Yes, I do."

"What colossal vanity!"

"I can't do without you."

"But I don't believe you love me either. Be honest."

"Oh love," Gerald said, "that isn't the point."

"It is for me." No, she thought. You need me as a sort of priestess, because you're too conventional to tote Monica round into the cornfields and under the trees. "Don't spoil things," she added kindly. "This can't be permanent, I'm not cut out for that sort of life. Why not just enjoy ourselves while I'm here and part friends? You'll find another girl, you know you will."

But all Gerald did was to tighten his arm round her waist.

"I don't believe you care two straws for your Oliver, I'll make you change your mind. You see," he said angrily.

"What's the time?" Juliet asked.

Monica looked up from the embroidery she was pretending to sew. "You're early back, you must've stepped on it. Where's Juliet?"

"Making tea. Would you like some? It's hot tonight, I'm having a whisky."

"No tea, let's go to bed." Gerald was frowning and with secret pleasure she diagnosed that he had been rebuffed. But in bed he curled round her and went to sleep at once.

He's worn out with making love to that girl, he's too old to manage two women any more, he doesn't love me, Monica thought, her turmoil returned. She hated his soft breathing, and the arm thrown over her shoulder was an insult.

19

Later that night the thunderstorm broke. Monica didn't wake up. The lightning flashes and crashing thunder mingled with her violent emotions and wove in with her dreams, driving her deeper into sleep. It was Gerald who heard the children crying and got up. As he shut the door gently behind him so as not to disturb her, a blinding flash of lightning flooded the corridor and lit up Juliet emerging from her room.

"Poor darlings, Harriet hates thunderstorms, and that sets off Martin," he said. "Don't worry, children, I'm coming."

"I don't care for this one much myself," Juliet said.

"Daddy shut the window so the lightning can't come in," Harriet begged.

"It won't hurt you," Gerald promised, but he shut the window and sat down on her bed.

Harriet hid her face on his chest. "I don't want to see it. Why won't it go away? Oh, oh!" The thunder rumbled again.

With every flash Martin jumped and shivered and buried his face in Juliet's bosom. The magnificence of the storm excited him, his fear was a pretext for nestling up, and he clutched and squeaked into her breasts, which were warm and faintly steamy from the hot night, intoxicating to smell.

Poor little sod, Gerald thought, he's all right, he's in love for the first time. It was Harriet who was really afraid. She sat stiff and upright and held his hand very tight, her face livid in the lightning flashes. She couldn't have borne the storm at all if Gerald hadn't been there. The thunder was a punishment for making magic. God was shouting from the sky.

"Harriet," Gerald said. "That crash was several miles away.

You can tell exactly where the storm is by counting between the flash and the thunderclap. Here we go." The room was alive with lightning. "A mile a second, 1, 2, 3, 4, 2, 2, 3, 4, 3, 2, 3, 4, 4, 2, 3, 4," he counted before the thunder roared. "Four miles. You try next time."

"That was only two!"

Next time thunder and lightning arrived together in a splitting crash.

"Right overhead," Gerald said calmly. "I wouldn't be surprised if there was a tree struck. In the morning we'll go and have a look."

"The house will be struck, we'll all be killed," Harriet said.

"Not at all probable. There are far too many trees taller than this house. The lightning will like them much better than the house to run down. Think, Harriet, how many hundred years this house has been standing here and what terrible storms it has come through perfectly safely."

Juliet found this idea a comfort herself.

"What you've got to remember about thunderstorms is that lightning goes for tall trees, so they're a good thing to have about, but the worst possible place to take shelter under."

Another colossal roll of thunder accompanied by brilliant lightning drove Harriet to cling to him like a terrified kitten with all its claws out. Gerald began to repeat the 23rd psalm.

"*The Lord is my shepherd* . . . Come on, say it with me, you know the words. You'll find it a great comfort in a tight corner when you're frightened."

Juliet listened.

"*Yea though I walk in the valley of the shadow of death I will fear no evil: for Thou art with me* . . ." He spoke the words quite as a matter of course.

"Daddy," Harriet said, "have *you* ever been really afraid?"

"Good Lord yes, often. Everyone is, some time or another, it's nothing to be ashamed of. Being brave is being frightened and not letting it pull you to pieces, carrying on just the same.

Count. The storm's beginning to move away."

When the rain came down Harriet's eyes closed. Gerald felt her hand relax and her fingers uncurl from his. As he laid her head carefully down on the pillow she unrolled into bed like a rag doll; he pulled up the sheet and tucked her in.

Martin had been asleep for some time, but Juliet, unwilling to disturb Harriet, had sat on, watching Gerald's face as it was lit up by the intermittent lightning. It was quite tranquil, suffused by calm confidence. He really does believe God walks beside him, she thought, wondering how a man could be so tenderly paternal and such a shyster both at once.

In silence he held the door open for her, and taking her elbow propelled her into her own room and shut the door behind them.

As long as the storm raged Monica slept, she was woken by the quiet. The heavy rain had stopped beating down, leaving nothing but the sound of unhurried dripping from the trees and gutters. The first thin light of dawn was beginning to creep into the sky.

"Gerald," she said and put out her hand. Not there. He must have gone to pee, she thought sleepily. Then she realised that his place in the bed beside her was cold.

"The children must've had a nightmare! Why didn't I hear?" With foreboding she got out of bed to go and find him. As she left the bedroom she saw him in the half light at the end of the passage, an outline against the window. In spite of the semi-darkness there was no doubt about it whatsoever: he was coming out of Juliet's room, not the children's. It was Juliet's door he'd just shut.

"You look like Lady Macbeth," he said. "Go back to bed. The storm's over and the children are asleep again. It was a real snorter, they were terrified poor darlings. I've just been seeing Juliet back across the passage, I think she was terrified too. Come on my love, don't stand there, I'm getting cold."

Cold? Monica's heart turned into a lump of ice. A perfectly

horrible non-feeling. She knew now what it was like for little Kay in the Hans Andersen fairy tale when his heart was frozen.

Sternly she said, "Don't lie to me."

"Wait till you feel my feet."

With her last fragment of consciousness Monica was aware that there was no Gerda to come and find her in the Snow Queen's palace and, with her tears, to thaw the frozen heart.

20

Rain had fallen all the morning. The children, confined
indoors, grew tired and quarrelsome. Unruffled, Juliet kept the
peace, the bloom on her not even dented. Monica noticed;
but found herself, with her rage rising, paradoxically glad to
have Juliet there to take them off her hands so that she could
concentrate on how to behave. Her balance was as precarious
as the top block on a child's tower of bricks.

By lunchtime she was exhausted with the effort to appear
normal. The suppressed self that for years had lain in wait,
merely pretending to be Mrs Webster, had taken over. The
understanding wife, the virgin in white, Daddy's good little
girl were all gone, supplanted by a maenad intent on making
Gerald suffer.

"You've got a headache *again*, Mummy," Harriet said.

"Not this time."

"You do look done up darling," Gerald said. "Why not
take it easy this afternoon? The rain's clearing, the children
can come with me round the farm to see how much storm
damage there's been. We'll take the station wagon, I want to
look at the corn. Go on children, you'll need your wellies. Are
you coming, Juliet?"

Of course she would. Monica watched while the party got
ready and the children ran out into the uncertain sunshine.
Juliet and Gerald walking towards the car looked married
already. Monica felt disembodied, not there at all.

But her heart was still beating. Juliet, Juliet. My place, my
place. He's a liar, a liar. There was the taste of bile in her
mouth.

The clock in the hall was speaking words from one of Martin's story-books. "Stick, stock, stone, dead."

Monica watched while the shell of herself laid the table and made the sandwiches, remembered to put out the cake and cover it with a teacloth.

"Stick, stock," the clock repeated.

Monica's shell made pastry, took out her sharpest knife and began to cut up steak and kidney to make a pie.

The high childish laughter came across the yard in a peal of mockery. In at the back door. Into the kitchen.

"The storm's done a lot of damage I'm afraid," Gerald said, "there's a whole field of corn laid. And there's an oak tree been struck in the paddock. We thought we heard it go last night, didn't we?"

He was laughing. We. The word stamped itself into his smile.

"If you haven't wetted the tea I'll have my bath first."

His smile became a jagged wound in his body.

Monica followed him upstairs with the knife in her hand and waited. Through a red mist she listened to the noises he was making in the bathroom: singing, splashing, brushing the rivulets of water off his body with his hands. He should lie, red too, at her feet, quite still with the smile wiped off. He must never have another woman. Her grasp tightened on the knife as the bath began running out.

From somewhere there was a voice. Slowly, as if from a long way away, words formed in her mind. Juliet's voice.

"Monica, I've had a telegram, I'm terribly sorry but it means I'll have to go. As soon as possible—"

For what seemed endless time Juliet watched the mask in front of her, the eyes staring out of black pits, the mouth a round hole. She saw recognition coming back into Monica's face. Monica's hand opened and the knife fell.

In front of Monica veil after veil was splitting down the middle with the noise of tearing silk, and then, suddenly, her eyesight was normal and the evil vision left her. The two women stared into each other's blanched faces. Juliet knew, and Monica knew she knew, that murder had been averted. The accusation in Juliet's eyes was like the judgement of heaven, but she was grateful for it. Now that someone saw her as she really was, with her darker self, she could never be quite so alone again.

The shattered pieces of her personality began to coalesce like spilt bits of mercury running together.

"Not bad news?" she said stiffly.

Juliet was trying not to vomit, not to run. Under her veneer Monica was old and ugly.

"No. As a matter of fact Oliver's back again."

"Go when you like. Tonight? It would be best if you did."

She looked down, unable to stand Juliet's gaze any longer, and saw the knife on the floor between them. Her knees gave out. She couldn't pick it up.

Her thoughts moved like snails. Running off to her boy friend! She hadn't even cared about Gerald.

At this moment Gerald came out of the bathroom naked except for the towel round his waist and fully conscious of the splendid figure he made. To find both his women in the bedroom together was a good beginning to the regime he hoped to institute. He smiled first at one, then the other.

"You lied," Juliet said to him sternly, "you lied." She picked the knife up and walking past Monica put it tidily on the dressingtable. "I don't ever want to speak to you again." Then she went downstairs.

Gerald unwound the towel from his loins.

"Juliet's going," Monica said, "she's had a telegram. From her boyfriend I think."

He kissed her on the cheek. "They're all the same except for you. They're a bore in the end, they don't know how to behave." But he couldn't keep the hurt out of his voice. "What on earth's that knife doing there? You'd better take it down to the kitchen before one of the children gets hold of it and cuts their fingers off."

'He didn't see,' Monica thought, 'he doesn't know what's happened, he's suffering from shock over Juliet.' She wanted to sit down because of her knees shaking. She was numb with shock herself.

"Tea's *ready*, Mummy," Harriet shouted up the stairs.

It was during tea that it came to Monica by what a hairs-breadth she had been saved, and what from. She thought she was going to faint, and put her head in her hands.

"You *have* got a headache."

"No. I'm better. After tea I'll read to you. Juliet, you'll need your wages if you're going to catch a train tonight." Not a minute longer in this house please God, not with those eyes reflecting her sin hour by hour. "I'll go and get them for you."

Harriet smiled.

Martin looked anxiously round the table. The only person who seemed at all happy was Juliet, and even he could see that she was miles away.

The telegram had said "Turkey no go. Please come," with a London address and telephone number. "I'll wash up, then I'll be leaving," she said.

Gerald hovered behind in the kitchen after the others had left. Juliet ignored him.

"You're not going tonight, are you?"

"You lied to me. About Monica. You said she didn't mind. She does. Terribly. You should watch your step."

But Gerald only smirked, and raising her arm she smacked his face with all the strength she had. His hand shot to his cheek and he looked at her the way Martin did, desolate and bewildered. But she only ran away upstairs to pack.

She said no goodbyes and no one saw her leave. Monica was putting the children to bed and Gerald was in the lavatory, waiting for the red mark on his face to fade. For a moment he felt a prisoner—of his house, his caste, even his wife. The only freedom he could ever have known was flying away from him up the drive. But the knowledge was too much to live with; he put it out of his mind as he pulled the plug.

The spotted cuckoo was singing its strangled parting cry but Juliet neither saw nor heard it. Her only thought as she hurried to catch the bus was 'Whose flat has Oliver managed to borrow? He's terribly good at managing.'

Having some time to wait for the London train she indulged in all the vices she knew would grate most in the environment she was escaping. She bought a woman's mag, the biggest wrapped chocolate biscuit she could find, a sausage roll and a can of Coca-cola.

The smell of British Rail waitingroom was nectar.

The train seemed desperately slow, but at least every second was taking her further from that seductive madhouse. Poor Gerald, seen in perspective he was really very ordinary; grotesquely so, Apollo as long as he was silent, but vocal, Bottom. To test her freedom she deliberately thought about his prick inside her and an involuntary spasm went through her body; but it had the same unreality as the memory of a dream. She strove to suppress her sexual debt to him; the only thing to keep in her mind was that he'd been sandy, and too pink. By the time the train reached the suburbs her holiday experience had dwindled away to a pawn to be set against Lucy.

Monica sat on the edge of Martin's bed. There were the streak marks of tears on his cheeks. Poor Martin, he'd been suffering from his first grand passion and she hadn't noticed. How little she knew about her children. Why should she expect to know when she hadn't known about herself?

"Why has Juliet gone away?" Harriet asked.

"Her boyfriend wanted her."

"Is she going to get married?"

"I don't know."

"Then why did she have to go in such a hurry?"

"People are always in a hurry if they're in love. Are you

153

sorry she's gone then?"

"Only quite. *I* think she was unkind."

"Oh? Why?"

"She didn't say goodbye to Martin."

Monica went downstairs and put on the best dinner she could contrive. Food was all she could think of to mitigate unhappiness. She realised just how much Gerald was mourning for Juliet when he came downstairs and was too dispirited even to decant a bottle of wine. She did it herself. 'We're both suffering,' she thought, 'and it's worse for him because he's innocent.'

But it was a silent meal, and both of them felt the dining-room was too large.

Monica sat at her dressingtable in front of the oval rosewood mirror, brushing her hair. What a pity it was short, the great point of long hair was that there was so much longer for thinking between the beginning and end of each stroke. The curtains had not yet been drawn; she looked out onto the moonlit garden as generations of Mrs Websters had done before her. The lawns bathed in moonlight appeared as cold as if there was a frost on the ground. She thought how the garden, covered up now with its summer frills, changed its shape through the year; but the structure underneath was always the same and in the winter its bones lay bare to see. The fountain at the heart of the design was fully unveiled.

But that design was good, hers was bad. She had just had her coverings torn off to show the bare bones of her nature in all their savagery. She would never be able to ignore them again. For the rest of her life she would have to live with that other self. But as the fountain playing for her down below never stopped all the year, holding the garden together round it, so the fountain of her love for Gerald linked her two natures and would never change. Poor Gerald, she'd seen his feet of clay. But what of it? There was something lifegiving in him that she would love for ever.

It was no use denying that while in the last fortnight she had, emotionally, travelled a thousand miles, Gerald had remained on exactly the same spot. When he had recovered from this setback she could look forward to numbers 22, 23 and so on ad infinitum, till the day arrived when he was past it and no woman would have him. 'I must do something about it well in advance,' she decided, 'or he'll never be able to bear it. And nor will I. I shall have to channel him into local government like his grandfather. I must have been mad to think he'd ever leave me, not for anyone.' She saw, like a weight on her breast, his pathological need for her. In a way he was a perpetual child, younger than Martin or Harriet.

As for Juliet, she was of no more importance than a swallow, come and gone again, streaking away to a better climate having taken what she wanted from this one; neither made nor prepared to stand its winter rigours. In an odd way her escape gave Monica pleasure for both of them. But no my girl, you'll never make a nest in this home.

The bedroom door opened. Out of the corner of her eye she saw Gerald reflected in the glass. He was not wearing pyjamas, he often didn't in summer. He stood behind her and she felt his erection hard against the small of her back.

"Come to bed," he said.

All the strength went out of her arm and she put the hairbrush down on the dressingtable before it could fall on the floor.

Moonlight flooded the carpet, but the tapestry bed curtains with their leaping harts lapped them round.

"You're the only woman who understands me," he said. "I couldn't live without you. Poor Juliet, she was a bit of a puritan."

"Look Gerald. This time I don't want to hear at what point in her sexual education she drew the line. I'm fed up. I asked you not to have her, and you did. What's more I know you lost your head over her and now you're unhappy because she's gone; so don't pretend. You'd've liked to keep her here as a sort of sub-wife, wouldn't you?"

Gerald said nothing.

"I don't mind how many women you have, but not in this house, not in our nest. And don't ever lie to me again."

"Now Juliet's gone must we still have that ghastly fellow Simon in?" Gerald said.

"I'm sick of the word Juliet. You can try and see if you can please your wife for a change."

But he had never failed to do this.

For a moment, an unfamiliar edge on Monica's voice worried Gerald. Then the warm reflection flooded over him that this was not an outsider, however desirable, but his wife, chosen and groomed by himself, the mother of his line, the repository of his life and love. There was nothing about her he didn't know. Of course she was a bit miffed.

Relieved that there was no longer any secret between them, he took his comfort as he always did.

Monica was watching herself, nervous in case what had happened would ruin her pleasure with him in bed.

It made no difference.

'Nothing will ever break us up,' she thought. 'Sexually we match completely. And what's more we're the tops. A couple of pros. I should have had it out with him in the first place. The whole thing need never have happened.' It hurt her to have to admit Simon had been right. But after all he was never going to know. No one was. 'No one except me.' That was at once her consolation and her penance.

And because she must wall up her destructive self, bring something new into her life to assuage her loneliness, to take her mind off the knowledge that Gerald would never change, she left out her diaphragm. Perhaps with another baby she could have a better understanding than she'd managed with her other two.

It was raining, soft early morning rain with a hot day on the way behind it. Harriet lay quietly in bed, savouring her privacy. No Granny. No Juliet.

When the rain stopped, before anyone else was awake, she

went out into the wet orchard and half in triumph, half in
terror, dismantled her magic and threw the wilted flowers
away.